VILLAGE PRODIGIES

"*Village Prodigies* uses a modest American town and its citizens to ponder an immodest array of the world's most baffling imponderables. Beginning with the fallibility of one's own internal compass — the mind — and extending to every further layer of reliable knowns (family, circle of friends, town, country, world), Jones's characters have been thrown a gauntlet of conflicts (personal, local, national). And if the inner world trembles with uncertainty, the physical world — by season, by tool, by history, by progress — plods forward regardless. The book has it both ways, showcasing the lyric beauty of the eternal and abiding, as well as celebrating the individual in his headlong hurl through the too-brief and chaotic corporeal life. I applaud the truly avant-garde nature of this project."

—**ANTONYA NELSON**, author of *Funny Once* and *Nothing Right*

"There is a novelistic wholeness, with characters recurrent and developing, and a firm sense of place, which, taken together, cause the sense of entering into a whole life. The drama and individuals are compellingly present. Nobody gets lost in the interweaving or in the shifts of perspectives . . . Some of the events are almost too painful to face, some too funny to do anything but grin. It is a fable as strong and true as that film I love, *Stand by Me,* but with the grim future we all have also hovering in every instant."

—**DAVE SMITH**, author of *Hawks on Wires* and *Little Boats, Unsalvaged*

"It's one of the best contemporary poetry books I've ever read ever. The book plays with different forms, plays with punctuation and lines, syntax and diction, varies the points of view, moves between comic and tragic. It makes the poems continually surprising both in form and content, which also creates a lot of energy . . . A tremendous achievement."

—**STEPHEN DOBYNS**, author of *Cemetery Nights*

"This is a major thing, this here [book]. *Spoon River Anthology* on steroids and LSD."

—**T. R. HUMMER**, author of *Skandalon*

VILLAGE PRODIGIES

RODNEY JONES

A Mariner Original
MARINER BOOKS
Houghton Mifflin Harcourt
Boston   New York
2017

WWW.HMHCO.COM

Library of Congress Cataloging-in-Publication Data is available.

ISBN 978-0-544-96010-7

Book design by Mark R. Robinson

PRINTED IN THE UNITED STATES OF AMERICA

DOC 10 9 8 7 6 5 4 3 2 1

In Memoriam

Kent Haruf
1943–2014

C. D. Wright
1949–2016

Memories are killing. So you must not think of certain things, of those that are dear to you, or rather you must think of them, for if you don't there is the danger of finding them, in your mind, little by little. That is to say, you must think of them for a while, a good while, every day several times a day, until they sink forever in the mud. That's an order.

Samuel Beckett, from "The Expelled"

CONTENTS

THE PORTAL OF THE YEARS

Whole days try to crowd into the portal. It is a portal or it is a switch-board. A big party line, each must wait a turn. Inchoate twittering of porch chickens. Rain barrels full after the storm empties. A small place, everyone speaks and everyone listens. Though in the portal, it is not places but times that converse, while inside the switchboard, it is only the one time. Early summer, a barber in the front room shakes talcum onto the neck of a janitor. An operator named Eunice places the calls, and they race through the feet of crows. Eunice overhears everything: she can describe the new baby's crib-cap, the voices of father and son raised in anger before the shooting in the motel room. But omniscience is discreet, nods knowingly, chews gum. God imagines nothing. A man kneels to the meat on the grill and knows the unsayable thing. She has been dead weeks and the Zippo she slipped into his pocket still makes a flame.

BOOK ONE

REQUIEM FOR REBA PORTIS

I *(Cleon Portis)*

Deaf raconteur will talk your ear off
(just a loose reckoning, the ratio
of saying to listening might
run anywhere from 80:20 to 97:03)—

the children wait, sort, analyze.
Then respond on a yellow legal pad.
He reads quickly and never replies.
They do not expect explanation.

These are anecdotes, after all, and in each
some especially vivid or sentimental
image: the theft of a slave's only socks,
a hole in the woods with no bottom.

The lung sounds in his words click home.
A gravel road winds past a quarry.

The house sits on a limestone bluff
between a spring and a cemetery.

Today the daughter is very happy
and writes to tell the father why.
After much phoning, she has found
a capable girl to stay with mother.

The father has a way of making himself
handsome when he does not wish
to reply; it is the look of a good boy
who has been gifted a pony with one eye.

The eyebrows rise, the head tilts
like a bobber when a bream nibbles
but will not take the hook. This
is Morse a new anecdote is forming.

A cousin previously unknown to him
has written from Texas she wants to see
the old homeplace and will visit
once she gets out of the penitentiary.

Well, it is a hard kind of thing to answer.
Brooke looks to Cleon and Cleon to Brooke.
White in her wingchair the mother taps.
Seth debrides anecdotes that concern him.

From visit to visit, anecdotes cycle
like painted horses on a carousel.
In one, sailors fish for monster catfish
in the mouth of the Amazon. The bosun

fashions a hook from a steel piston.
The cook proffers a whole chicken for bait.
Another is of a widow and son,
cotton pickers — once the mother

questioned the way he sold it. What
was that word she used? *Untoward*.
And how can she forget now?
His voice drags a tarred sack. At intervals

the widow undoes her blouse,
and the son, who is so tall he stands
flatfooted to nurse, wears
a rooster feather in his hat.

II

Seth Portis deconstructs his mother

as he reads Gerald Edelman's *Wider Than the Sky*
to better comprehend dementia

(meat electronics, neural pathways
from thalamus to cortex,
redundancy loops) — her challenges

with latency and recency — as if
the portal in which the present self

regards the past has been altered
or reversed. Things

tessellate and do not agree.
Many times exchange places in the portal.

The lights snap on 3 a.m.
He raises up from sleep

and there stands Reba, white-gowned, ghostly,
and bright-eyed, eighty-two,

some pain low in her right side:
"I may need to go to the emergency room.

It may be appendicitis. I know
I'm not pregnant.

I haven't been exposed."

III

It is how we see time that composes us and marks us as the most
intelligent species.

On any one day, with any given person, intelligence varies.

On only one afternoon might Keats pen "Ode to a Nightingale." On
only one night could Monk unblock the grand piano and deliver the
chords of " 'Round Midnight."

When Reba says, "Something is wrong with the present or me," it plays
a chord.

That Reba expresses some awareness of her dementia plays into
Brooke's hope that the good days—when mother summons the spirit to
go out to the flower bed and untangle crabgrass from the zinnias—
may proliferate.

Good days are optimized by desire. Bad days are inward days. Brooke must bring out Reba.

She prays. She reads books, studies articles. In time, designs a game, Name That Ancestor. Cold Springs rules. Daughter deals to mother from shoebox album.

Two decks, like gin rummy or canasta: the Portises, backcountry genteel, duded and frocked for picnics; the Dunlops, parvenus in overalls and floral, seed-bag dresses.

Hope is familiar at this stage of the disease. Mother identifies among the Portises two sets of double first cousins, the Hungarian aunt most take for Creek.

Win after win: Rose, Peach, Anaximander.

In the Dunlop five-generation photo, she names each face with the presbyopic focus of hill people, which may count as miracle or symptom.

Seventy years ago is closer than the past ten minutes.

I V

The strong stuff when the lid is taken off:
"Who are you?" or "That old man is not

my husband!" Aphasia's grapes, target

thought, itch she could not put her finger on —
"Not Reba," friends said, "bless her heart."

And the children dismayed, estranged: for now
she would sull up, and now cuss a blue streak

who had always been so staid in polite company,
so coiffed, white-glove and Sunday-school proper.

Of parents, children know which is meaner, which
brighter, who more likely to forget.

But one day, foraging among the freezer's
bearded cutlets, the daughter found a hidden bra.

And said the word. Father delayed. Son thought no—

he still had hope when a neighbor asked her, "What
kind of woman would I be?" and she answered, "Ugly."

But her questions shrank to platitudes;
blue doubts circled her. When she began

to ask, the doctor said, "If you know
enough to ask, you don't have it."

V

They would be happy if you told them every night
the dark master of inappropriate sobriety
climbs the rungs of the Las Vegas hell
of the early-twenty-first-century Calvinists,
shakes off hell's ashes, and has a nip
of the really powerful stuff with their mother.

Waking with a jeweler from Buenos Aires
the morning after bringing down the house
by singing every verse of "Hey, Good Lookin',"
she could revise her comportment and sober up.

Oh, they know evil is just like she said
and never what you think at first.
You have to remember sin
before you can turn it into something else.
It is just a neurofibrillary tangle
or a random amyloid beta deposit.

And this is why she hears voices
and rain when there is no rain,
why she wakes in a clammy sweat
after midnight and insists
that she is not where she is and wants to go home.
And all their father does is pull on his coat and trousers and take her
on a long ride three times around the circle drive. And says,

"I am glad we are home."
And she, "Oh, me too!"
before he turns off the lights,
smiles, and locks the doors.

VI

But one night she bolts — no one knows
until the ambulance brings her home,
mud on her nightgown, lespedeza hair,
and the next day the children arrive
to arrange for a caregiver.
But their father is adamant: "No,
I will take care of her." A note,
a no; a note, an anecdote. The battle

of the spoken and the written
ends usually with the voice,
but here the witness comes
from Kingdom Hall, and stays, and divides
into a trinity: apparently selfless,
pregnant beauty, the black,
heretofore unacknowledged cousin.
The medications, the daily bath,
the bimonthly perm.

The mother at the end of the world,
not the end of the world. Witness
now this Godhead care, frank as prayer:
"Sit down, Mrs. Reba." Today's
special is green beans and tenderloin.
As she shall be known, she becomes
"I'll have what my husband's having,"
but one day, the way he looks at *her* —
it catches in the throat — "Who
are these people?" she shouts and will
not leave and stamps her fists on the table.

V I I *(Dedication)*

When you were first unrecognized
was that not a kind of freedom,

as you sat across from her

and she looked up
furtively but with a stern pique

until the Witness said, "Mrs.
Reba, this is Brooke, *Brooke*,

your daughter." Then zero. Every
A you earned to please her morphed to N

as you reverted to the suspicion
that she had always preferred your brother,

and thought, She *does* know *him*.
But something, the way she stared

at his glass, then hers, so you saw
for her, there was only one glass.

The blue glass you gave her,
she believed he had stolen.

VIII

"Funny disease" lacks nuance, complexity.
"Tragic" trots to the table and barks.
"Useless," they called Shep, the family dog.

But there are many useful ways to characterize dogs.

Her father, Black Jack Dunlap, sold Cadillacs.
When he was too drunk to see
just one road, he would prop
little Reba in his lap and let her steer.

Told Mr. Curtis Wilkerson

when he had left Eunice
and begun to court Rowena,

who would become Jimmy's mother,

she said, out of the blue,

perhaps as an incentive or warning,

"I know I shouldn't say it, but sometimes I like it when love hurts."

They were drinking Crown Royal,

probably in the old Noble Arms Motel

that burned to the ground in '77,

when he started the funny business,

a hand at first, then lips,

and when she wouldn't have it,

"But you slept with Earl!"

"Oh, that. Earl was different. Earl cried."
And so he hit her, hard, and laughed.

IX

In a normal conscious state, individuals experience *qualia*, the presence in each mind that renders myriad details into one image. For some, in time, *qualia* disintegrate, details overlap. A resonance of images going to metaphors, a fluency of errors, a challenge for scientists; for Reba and Jack, memory is the flawed map that by following, they are bedazzled.

In the remembered present, Reba, the old woman, is a schoolgirl waiting to be picked up by her father in 1935:

> Ranting, cussing —
> in cuffs they take

him from the diner
and do not tell him

what he's done.
They do not say

which man he is
and he does not know.

                    X

The knobs removed from the faceplate,
the plug taken out of the wall.
No more the yeasty chateau
of dough and cinnamon
the daughter called *hotel soap cake*,
no more the son's gravy,
fried chicken, and greens.
And although she followed to a T
the teachings of Benjamin Spock,
she swore, "I will not be a human dairy,"
so never a memory of nursing.

Coffee she served them as children.
Sometimes dump salad,
jury-rigged from whatever
was freshly picked
and lying around the house.
More often cornbread and milk:
the milk in spring after the cows got out,

the onion she made them lick,
before drinking,
to mask the taste of bitterweed.

XI

The talk that she would be better dead—
if she hears it, she gives no sign,
eyes shut, head down, ruminative,
who once said, "Poor Margaret Stubbs,"

and "Promise, never let me get like that,"
and this is how it feels to come to life—
marooned or lost, creased and wadded,
a receipt blowing through a closed mall:

adrift on a gold-brown leather recliner,
the little finger of her left hand tapping
on the crocheted antimacassar,
palpebral twitches of chronic hypnagogia.

And also in some frail potency of long ago
the ice block slides down the chute
into the steel vat, bang, and she opens
eyes, looks around, and smiles wildly.

Goes back through the portal, the variable
ruin of experiences. The house, the barn.
And returns with water from a dry well
or the damp heat of some lost argument.

While the Witness rubs cream into her back

and watches *Jeopardy!,* and the strange
old gentleman, her husband, naps,
she skips, often with a cat or a dog.

Today she drags a doll to the crib
of 1926 or '27 and holds forth
to this corn-eyed sock coquette
on the importance of being moral.

Cobwebs in every corner, sneezedust
in slatlight, golden and granulated
through the latched feed door —
bad girl, she says, thump-thump-thumps.

Do not touch yourself down there
and when she is good and satisfied
the coquette has returned to infancy,
unbuttons her shift to nurse, coos

O little playmate, come out and play with me —
rat-rattling behind her in the cornhusks,
cows trance-chewing hay long rotted —
"Mrs. Reba, button yourself back up."

She starts up to leave, the Witness
buttoning her shift, repeating "Mrs.
Reba" — in the aisle of the barn
she hears her mother calling "Reba!"

the bell clanging in the wellhouse.
"Don't make me go cut a switch!"
Reba Dunlap would like to go
to the house now, but the bull blocks her.

XII *(Cleon)*

Hyperthymesiac nonagenarian can forget nothing
counting out pills placing them in her mouth
kisses on school buses in cars up logging roads

the yellow pill is for anxiety the blue pill opens
all mouth all legs sprinting to his taxi in a nightgown
the war over he had taken the train from Seattle

one red pill one night after second shift let off
the land paid for the children away at college
her body Dread Mills said like a Coca-Cola bottle

now she stays on an island it is all a right smart
different now where there was a field mark void
she does not remember Jehovah's Witnesses lift her

there are four rows of trays in the pill organizer
the trays are yellow blue red and lavender
one year her hair went white as Washington's

her lips reassemble in the lips of grandchildren
was there a storm clouded yes she said yes
all of it at once she would give him everything

the exclusive breasts the intelligent hands pills
each pill a steppingstone by which he would reach her
as the stones erode dim and vanish into the water

BROOKE PORTIS

Cutting pineapple upside-down cake for parents' seventieth anniversary. Daddy's fine after neck surgery. Always such a positive attitude! but mother, please pray for her, like she's gone but still here, never knowing who or where, all day waiting for a ride home from school, all night singing, We'll understand it bye and bye.

MAVIS BLACK

Anniversaries and birthdays are always hardest. Will call later. Meant to catch you in church, but had a bug. On my way to see Courtney. LAX just confiscated my hair gel.

DOROTHY GREEN CHALMERS

One of the most precious women God ever created! She's not gone. She's practicing for the Hallelujah Choir!

JAMIE LEE BUCKELEW

She taught u so much. Can't imagine how much you miss her. It has been 20 years and I still miss her. The good thing is we both have wonderful memories.

MARTHA McCOY

She loved to set on her porch and watch us work in the garden. Weather we were hoeing gathering beans, or planting squash. She would wave every time I went past.

XIII *(Redundancy Loops)*

Something bowed up in her she would not take back.
Things flew all over her or rubbed her the wrong way.

One day when the son was too cavalierly mowing the lawn
(the world-canceling noise of the mower

had accommodated an inner Albert Hall
where he was channeling Chuck Berry),

shaking like a dog climbing out of a pond
as he hopped on one leg and jigged the mower/guitar

ahead of him in the glorious riff
that made the trees by the cemetery take off their shirts,

she saw him, she saw what he was not,
came up from behind, and grasped him, firmly, by the occiput

before she spoke of his future, employing lubricants
like "elbow grease" so he would not forget.

He leapt up. He fired the other musicians. He caught the train.
He boarded the plane and flew back to the United States.

Why does anyone remember anything?
She had on a whirlaround-skirt-and-shorts set,

and after she let him know just what kind of person he was,
she flung off the skirt, grabbed the handle of the mower,

and took off with the mind to show him.
Then he saw. She had forgotten the shorts.

She was mowing in her panties. He did not know how to feel.
He ran behind her with the skirt and tapped her on the shoulder,

but she would not stop. Even when he shouted "Mother"
(and later she would ask to hear the story and laugh)

she would not stop, and he saw, she would go around and around.
There would only be that moment until she had erased the pattern,

and he stood back, and thought of the seasons, and thought,
The fear of the mother is the beginning of memory.

———————————————————————————

(2010–2014)

THE SECRET ORDER
OF THE EAGLE

XIV *(The Stutterer Seth Portis)*

Sweet tooth, goldilocks, apple
of his mother's stink-eye, desperate
for attention, but too shy
to cry when the blacksmith
grabs and swings him by his ears,
he takes solace in the swaddling
roar of the party that conceals him.
When he follows the older kids
to play hide-and-go-seek,
he sneaks back. All ears.
He never cries near
big people. He listens.
He does not learn.
He becomes them.
The way they drink iced tea

when the game draws close,
and when the noise
goes deeper in the woods,
they switch to beer.
He sees how, when they speak,
they forget each other.
It is his favorite game. Hide-
and-go-seek. He does not need
to be discovered to know
he will be It. It is
his special power, invisibility.
He is only famous
while hidden.

XV

Fat little Dudley chanted his name and printed it in block on his binder cover:

at first, just MANN;

and later — on books, on baseball gloves, on biceps and oaks —

BIG MANN

Prefecture, license, leverage, mode that carried him.
He marked its heft and shine up close,

the way it gripped the road and cornered: a champagne
Jaguar, a yellow Harley, chopped

with raised chrome handlebars. He drew

the sleekness of the seat and gas tank, specular
pipes curving from the manifold. And saw

his name flash as if published on storefront glass:
the aviators, the Nazi helmet; and girls behind

him, each day a different girl—some blond,

some black—each a lens that made him larger,
but each a little less like mother. Calling "Dudley, Dudley—"

she could hear him when he got like that, explosion
after explosion since his father passed. Like he was steel.

Sometimes she said she thought he was a motor:

one gear, no going back, no change as he got older.
He grew and sang the mash. He sang the monster mash.

XVI *(On a Warm Day in Late July, in the Lot Across from Cleon Portis's*
Barn, Lonely Luck, Seth Portis, Jawaharlal Mills, Mack Mack,
Dudley Mann, and George Brown Play Pitch, Discuss What Is on
Their Minds Regarding a Book by J. Edgar Hoover, Arrive at a
Fateful Decision to Form a Club, Decide to Refer to Each Other
by Last Names Only, and Swear a Blood Oath)

Observe that the ball they toss is the center of a regulation ball, wrapped tightly in kite string and covered with electrical tape.

That the position of each boy in the circle and who throws to whom is a matter of health and personal security.

That, on the recommendation of Lonely Luck and Seth Portis, who have checked out every book in the Cold Springs Elementary School Library, each boy has attempted to read J. Edgar Hoover's *Masters of Deceit: The Story of Communism in America and How to Fight It.*

That Jawaharlal Mills would prefer *The Giants of Science,* that Dudley Mann tends to detective fiction.

That Mack Mack reads *Lou Gehrig: Pride of the Yankees,* and George Brown *The Island Stallion.*

That the library is small, that, behind the atlases, Lonely Luck has discovered a picture of Gina Lollobrigida in *Pageant* magazine and often imagines a log cabin on a dude ranch where she stands in the door in a black net appliquéd with stars, invites him inside, and says, "Thelonious, you are such a *wone-dare-fool* reader. Would you like to see my breasts?"

That the patriotism of fourth-grade boys is every feather as absurd and elegant as the mating displays of peacocks.

Thus, all had agreed, if reluctantly, to read the book, and now the idea of dangerous secrets is in the air: the ball goes round the circle, according to each boy's disposition and makeup. A hard vector from Mack to Mann; a slow loop of cousin love from Mann to Mills; a putted shot or wounded duck from Mills toward Brown; from Brown to Luck, a thank-you note; from Luck to Portis, a sidearm sling with English on it; and when Portis winds up and raises his leg, Mack begins to run.

The idea of abundant and omnipresent criminal conspiracies and organizations bounces, too, and hits the mark, sails true, or out of control. It's Mann's idea to use last names; Luck suggests the agency, the NST; Mills the club's overall purpose and structure; and Mack, the blood oath. "On pain of death," they chant as the ball goes round. They have agreed, they cannot stop to make the cuts until the ball goes once undropped around the circle. Near dark, flapping and trailing a string, the ball grows hard to see, the boys draw closer. It is not a good ball, but it is Portis's ball.

A. Petite smells like lard biscuits, basset hound, and wood smoke.

B. Redheaded with freckles, will bite.

C. Take off the hat, cowboy.

D. Supernumerary nipples.

E. Head too small for body.

F. Go to the bathroom and wash off the mascara, raccoon.

G. Nine years old, one hundred thirty-seven pounds.

H. Round face, leg brace, orthopedic shoes.

I. Pledge of Allegiance early-onset priapism.

J. Holds hands with first cousin on bus.

K. May I please go be excused? Number two.

L. Are you a boy or a girl?

M. Beaten last night with bicycle pump.

N. Final warning. Don't bring your pet squirrel to school.

O. Stinky cottonhead with black molars.

P. White Bible, white shoes.

Q. Dead sorrel mare on conscience.

R. Shockboy the electric fence whizzer.

S. Will not use toilet at school.

T. One blue eye, one brown.

U. Thirteen, five-eight, thirty-nine minutes older than brother.

V. Stone Age, they call him.

W. Cross-eyed desk carver.

X. Pinch and skedaddle.

Y. Truck-stop whore's daughter.

Z. One step, twelve words.

XVIII

Thelonious Luck, band director's son,
the only boy in Cold Springs named for a pianist:
at three learning to read
from Li'l Abner *and* Pogo;
at five, stalled in the immoderate
distraction of his love
for the music teacher's daughter;
he survives the rigors of first grade
by relishing the surplus
of what he has already learned;
at seven, he prefers watching
his story for the contest
float down Mud Creek and sink
to the blue of a ribbon. He has transposed
two versions of polo from pony to bicycle.
At eight, when he leans over his desk
in the nodding stir
and ecclesiastical drone
of Geography lessons,
he draws up
from the smell of ancient spit
an image of Sacajawea
bathing in the Yellowstone
and pencils it firmly on the cover
of his Blue Horse notebook
along with Two Belly Buttons,
the single male child
of identical-twin mothers.

XIX

The club had to be big. Why else start a club?
And Bobby James Chalmers was the linchpin.
Portis had been contacted by the NST, he told Bobby,
regarding a matter of importance to the leader:
Certain objects—coat hangers, belts—had gone
missing from the cloakroom. The NST
had linked this to more serious criminal activity—
unsolved murders, counterfeiting, espionage.
Portis told Bobby only what he needed to know.
In coordination with the KNC, NST had requested
they form a special investigative unit:
code name Eagle; attachment priority, 3C.
For security reasons, they must use last names.
"NST has asked me to ask you to serve as Chief."
"Why me and not you?" asked Bobby. "Classified,"
Portis said. "Not everything they said is clear.
But I do know the NST considers IQ tests,
also personal hygiene and handwriting analysis.
Leadership is a gift, they said, it can't be taught,
but Communications Officer is important, too.
Knowing too much is always a danger to the Chief."
Bobby took this well. He hit Portis on the shoulder.
And proposed a race. They ran from the oak tree
to the backstop behind home plate and back again.
"Okay, I'm Chief," said Bobby. "It sounds like fun.
And since I've been saved, I've been thinking
about more than myself, about bearing witness."

Early organizational meetings presented challenges,
and time sneaked and gathered. A pair of galoshes
vanished from the cloakroom. The deputy sheriff
announced new leads in the Suggs murder case.
Intercontinental ballistic missiles pointed at the country.
They divided the class into quadrants. From Group A
they chose three citizen leaders. "Jawaharlal Mills," said Portis,
"is the best boy in our class." But Chalmers wanted George Brown.
"Excellent," Portis said. "And Mack Mack comes to mind."
"A patriot," said Chalmers. "What about Mills?" Portis asked.
"You can't trust Mills," Chalmers said. "He tried
to drown Amelia at camp." "That's just not true,"
Portis said. "Where's the evidence?" "He talks funny,"
Chalmers said. "Listen to the *s*'s. He's black Russian."
"That's ridiculous," Portis said. "He had a cleft palate."
But Chalmers wouldn't listen. They decided on Candy Dobbs,
not a bad choice. And it helped to have the inner council
at meetings. But there were other problems.
Chalmers wanted turquoise to be the official club color.
"Turquoise is too loud," Portis argued. "What about gray?"
"I've got it. Red," said Chalmers. "Red's in the flag."
"Red draws attention to itself," Dobbs said. "It sticks out."
"Let's don't fight. Let's settle it with a race," Chalmers said.
"According to the NST manual for secret organizations,"
Portis said, "it should be something we can use in code."
It went like that a while, and then a fortuitous suggestion:
"Let's pray," said Chalmers. "Jesus Christ will make it *clear*."

Near sundown, they climb the haystack in the barn loft. Bobby pushes up a sheet of tin and crawls out onto the roof. The tin slick and hot. In dread and scorn, Seth creeps while Bobby stands on his head at the apex, and cartwheels the horizon from one weathervane rooster to the other.

Bobby's father, Possum, leads the devotional in the living room before supper. Each child must say a Bible verse or no supper. "Each time," says Possum, "I read a Bible verse, something I've never thought occurs to me." Seth's is the fifth verse of the first chapter of Matthew: "And Salmon begat Booz of Rachab; and Booz begat Obed of Ruth; and Obed begat Jesse."

At the supper table, Possum thanks the Lord Jesus Christ this great nation is not communist; he asks that Mrs. Alice Milton be released from her grief; he prays for those in prison and sick and starving pagans in India; he thanks the Lord for the presence of Seth Portis in their house and asks that the Portis family be blessed, naming them all. When Seth cracks an eye to peep, the steam has stopped rising from the corn on the cob; Bobby's older sister, Sally, looks back at him, sticks out her tongue, points at her eyes, and shakes her head.

When the door to Bobby's bedroom shuts, they are Portis and Chalmers again. Chalmers says, "Portis, tell me about your contacts in Washington." "It all began," says Portis, "when I wrote a letter asking about how to design an entrance for a fallout shelter." "What does the NST stand for?" A knock at the door: Sally with the Monopoly box.

You can see a person's character in the way he plays Monopoly. Sally sits with crossed legs — red toenails, shortie pajamas — the banker, the interpreter of rules. Seth lands on Boardwalk and plays for Park Place. Bobby buys up the cheaper properties.

XXII

Woe to the six-year-old in public school
who knows more than high school teachers.

Petting infinity while his classmates cuddle Pooh,
he deduces the mass of the balance wheel

in the Mickey Mouse clock above the blackboard
by its ticking, and finds one day an enemy.

Who, for no apparent reason, shoves him
into a thorn, rubs compost in his face,
and pinches his testicles hard—

"Did you hate him?" "I did not hate him."

Prying open the portal of the years,
A Dr. Singh drives questions into Mills.

Until he makes out the friend between them.
And knows this third boy was husband,
he the wife, and the enemy the other woman.

"Was it simple, the attitude of your enemy?
Unforgivable to have wished him ill?"

"When they prayed for him, I was jealous."

That he lay in an iron lung. "Innocent,"
one man said. "I touched his face,
when they opened the casket, to confirm

that the corpse with bow tie and crew cut
was not faking death for the attention."

1. **Titles are important. Chief leaves no doubt.**
   Communications Officer, Secretary and Treasurer,
   Operations Director, Docent, First Major—
   Chalmers swears these in on his mother's Bible.

2. **It is essential to communicate privately.**

3. **In the ideal top-secret organization,**
   everyone should feel second in the order.
   "If the Chief is killed, be ready to take charge."
   Mack and Mann, because they are large,
   become Rovers. Luck the Scribe begins to write
   the names of Inspectors and Special Agents.
   Each receives certificates affixed with the NST seal,
   surveillance report forms, and evidence kits.
   That leaves the big dumb: knife throwers,
   smokers, and chewers: Deputies, Detectives.

4. **Keep potential enemies close: award them**
   certificates stamped *Extraordinary Honor*.
   After jujitsu training, Deputies patrol playground.
   Special Agents begin surveillance of cloakroom.

5. **Procedures are paramount, procedures and protocol.**
   Chalmers commands the Inspectors and Special Agents,
   who give orders to Detectives and Deputies.
   Above it all, Mann and Mack move
   from group to group and report to Luck.
   And one day Chalmers asks, "Where do *you* stand in the chain?"
   "The Communications Officer has no rank," says Portis.
   "He decodes NST orders and passes them on to the Chief."
   Portis shows him one, "Tiger ransacketh mulberry stack,"

and starts to explain, but Chalmers wants to race again.
Then, as suggested in the NST directive on protocols
for top-secret operations, Luck draws out on paper
the chain of command, memorizes it, and swallows it.

XXIV *(Culls)*

The uninvited, the ones with first names:
Billy and Mildred, retarded twins, once
held back, twice demoted; Dorothy — she
was always damp — they called her "the sweater."
Dougie, with holster, pistol, and cowboy suit —
he didn't run, he galloped; he didn't talk, he
neighed. Paul, the undertaker's son,
clunking with steel brace and orthopedic shoes;
Carl, who did impressions of Daffy Duck;
Warren, the ringleader of the big dumb;
Denise, who smelled of butt and camphor.
Not suspects. No reason to interrogate.

XXV

Ever since the welfare lady dropped them off,
people saw he was different from his brothers.
The same mother, some said, but different fathers.
But was he or wasn't he? The skin, those curls
in a valley where the Klan held public raffles.
But to see him work, a little boy like a man,
at seven, driving the pickup in the hayfields,

and him, left-handed, broom on the pedal.
Big for his age, smart, considerate of older people,
not like his brothers who hit the ground in trouble.
To see him throw a rock or run. He had a grace about him.
The sweetness to carry bags or open doors. Nervous —
people said every night he had bad dreams,
but he blended in. Cedric at first, then Mack.
Mack Mack. He was not black. He was adopted.

XXVI

Wednesday, September 14, commenced with announcements.
"The bake sale was a big success. The student of the week
is Amelia Fortenberry. Please do not write on your desks.
For morning recess, the line leader will be Eugene Balthrop;
for lunch, Geraldine Wiggers; for afternoon, Jawaharlal Mills.
Congratulations, sparrows! for winning third place
at the history fair for your model pioneer log cabin.
Welcome back, Candace! We hope you are feeling better.
The lunch menu today is sloppy joes, french fries, and green beans."
And here Mrs. Grimmer stops and removes her reading glasses.
"Children, someone in this class is not being a good citizen.
Ann Guilford left her new pink mittens in the cloakroom
on Wednesday morning. On Thursday they were not there."
Then silence that bristles with passed notes and secret looks.

Later, a question: "What is the county seat of Walker County?"
"It could not be more *clear*," said Chalmers, "that the county seat
of Walker County is Jasper. It is very *clear*." And at recess
the inner council convenes under the oak by the tennis court.

XXVII *(Suspects)*

1. Winona, because she doodled horses,
snowflakes, butterflies,
because her hair gleamed like a crow's feathers,
because of the shade of her skin,
because her lips did not move when she read
silently, because everyone knew
Japs were worse than communists,
Japs would kill themselves to win,
because she would not look
you in the eye, because her penmanship was perfect,
because she was from Hawaii.

2. Stanley, because he wore corduroy trousers
instead of dungarees, because
he carried buckeye balls to ward off colds
and had the ugliest ears in class,
because his nose bled, because he talked
through his nose with a northun brogue
when he read his report on "Abraham Lincoln,
Our Greatest President," because he was seen
coming out of the cloakroom he might
have stolen the coat hangers, because he smelled
like kerosene and Vicks VapoRub, because
he was cross-eyed, had impetigo, because
he was a Jehovah's Witness, because no one
had ever heard of him before he came from Ohio,
and in all the fourth grade the only boy
with a brown flap hat and an orange plaid coat.

XXVIII *(Recess)*

Will it be the same forever, summoned by the bell,
joy in the morning, terror of the afternoons
graven in the scour of bald patches that stretch
from the facing lines of the patty-cakers
to the black-market ditch where Warren sells cigarettes?

Under the oak, Chalmers calls the meeting to order.
The citizen leaders give brief reports
and then vote in the last recruits.
Portis begins the NST directive. "Consider all . . ."
as a ball rolls through and they pitch it back.

And perhaps because Portis has a fever, sees
for an instant, in the deep scoop shoes
have rutted out beneath the swings, an eye.
The eye floats inside the sole of a foot.
But gone, the foot and eye, the day whirls black.

And lost among the kicked balls, the inmate
who cannot read, released from the tyranny
of books and lessons, twists a skinny arm,
and beside the one who races her own shadow,
the stalker and the stalked come to terms.

And the tiny brilliant boys who see the future
and swear when they are big they will remember
the injustices, and the girls who prize fairness
forsake in the amnesia of games their Jesus
and drive hard to knock the air out of the ball.

XXIX *(The Coup)*

Count backwards from ten
to where memory stops.
The numbness of ether leaves
at the center of the brain
a sneezing demon
Portis feels when the nurses
repeatedly call his name
to draw it burning out of him.

Portis lives. The doctor holds
up like plum preserves
the valedictory tonsils in a jar.
Ice cream, ginger ale,
five days of visits:
it is an open room, the pride
that follows suffering.

But something like a changed lock
when he comes back:
Mack and Mann nod,
shrug, and walk away.
Mills won't meet his eye.
After lunch, Chalmers
approaches and bows.

"Congratulations, Portis.
In your absence, the NST
contacted me. Mills helped
decode the message:

Lamb bath mulberry stack—
"I am now Communications
Officer. You are Chief."

x x x

A horse is not a human. A boy is not a woman.
And still one day a fox sits down with a farm girl;
a female magpie looks at a man and starts their nest.

The Shetland colt with pinkeye
that George Brown bottle-fed
and coaxed with apples and sweet feed
to rear and drink with its front hooves
firm on his shoulders was going to be a grown pony.

Didn't he know what it was:
an average specimen of a questionable breed
marketed by Sears, Roebuck to impersonate the dreams
of the North American kinder-cowboy nobility?
He was not an idiot child.

Only that for a few weeks, though the prospects
of interspecies communion admittedly diminished,
he nursed the odds
it might yet learn to count to twelve
or say Parcheesi.

Then, of course, it turned. That he taught it to rear,

that the lady got hurt—
it was not the boy's fault;

he had meant
to preserve its spirit.
A lesson for everyone,
quoth the preacher, about
mixing and good intentions.

XXXI

The new era starts like this. The class
studies clouds. "Thelonious, describe
the day for us," says Mrs. Grimmer.
"A little wispy," he answers, "a few
examples of cirrus and stratocumulus,
but mainly *clear*, I would say *clear*."
Under the oak, Portis calls the meeting to order,
citizen leaders give brief reports,
and Chalmers recites directives:
1. Do not believe the claims of suspects
when they claim they do not know;
they know, or we would not be interrogating them.
2. Citizen leaders must be Christians.
3. Disagreements may be settled by a race.
Dobbs worried, she said; things moved so slowly.
But in their last communiqué, the NST,
Chalmers told her, had expressed pleasure
with the performance of the new Chief
and upgraded their attachment priority to 2B.
"Consider all the evidence," said Brown.
"No fact is too small. Strands of hair,

leaf prints caught in boots.
Don't jump to conclusions. Warren
is fat, but not because of cakes and pies.
His father ate like that and never gained
a pound. There is a thyroid
problem on his mother's side."

XXXII

The big dumb run in taunting circles.
Each day they circle closer.
Winona swings, high
and higher, legs up at the peak—
Warren runs under her—a scream.
And this is not nothing, Portis:
this bump that sways the balance,
so the rope twists and snaps
until there's no place left to grip.
Mostly, when damage happens, no one
has to give the order. You do not
have to want a person hurt
to see her prone in the mud,
blue dress puckered in a bunch
around her waist, arm scrunched
at such an odd angle before
her eyes open and she sees
the faces gather around her
as the men lift her on the gurney
and tote her to the ambulance.

No crime here, these are children,
little children who did this thing
which they thought would please someone.

XXXIII

"What is this business with last names?"
the principal asks when he calls
the children to his office
in groups of three and four and starts
each time by clearing his throat and showing them
his green strap canvas belt.

"A girl is in the hospital."
He whacks it on his hand, withdraws
from the fob pocket of his trousers
a stopwatch, looks each in the eye and says,
"When I push the button you will have one minute:
tell me how this started and who all is involved."

"That girl wouldn't hurt a fly."
He waits. He whacks his belt. All morning
watching them and taking notes.
And sees the ones with least to say who say the most,
and the almost guilty stifling their sobs
into yawns — he presses

silence on denials, arrives by dribs and drabs at facts
(the NST directives, chain of command),
then asks, "What is the meaning of this club?"
Like drying paint, this moment before

"Mr. Mills, Mr. Luck, you may leave.
Master Seth Portis, what *were* you thinking?"

XXXIV

A talking-to, a whipping with the belt—
To be a little boy again, Seth
—a whittling down to be a Seth—
His essay will be removed from the contest.
And he must resign as class president.
Write in your notebook one thousand times
"I will respect and love my classmates
and listen to what they have to say."
But fourth-grade crucifixion takes many forms:
less the talkings-to than the silent looks,
less the chase across the playground
than being caught, the big dumb laughing,
fists pecking at his balls like beaks,
and, later, Bobby James praying for him
the day before Halloween—
already he has carved fangs for his new mask.
Last year he was Pirate Jack.

(1955–1959)

REVERSALS OF FORTUNE

XXXV

When the second specialist had confirmed the opinion of the first, and
it became clear that Portis would die soon and in great pain,

and after he had called doctor friends to procure anodynes to silken the
wheels in the conveyors of the crematorium

and made what arrangements might be made discreetly regarding burial
vault, memorial service, and assorted legal dispensations,

and before he had informed wife, children, or close friends,
he found online, for a reasonable price, a beautiful mahogany coffin.

And the next day, another, of admirable plainness and simplicity.
And on Wednesday, for a mere $1,200, a third,

with carved wooden handles, hand-rubbed nitrocellulose finish, and
book-matched, quartersawn panels — they called it "the Lakeside"—

Soon he was noticing a dizziness on stairways, sometimes an enigmatic fluttering of the inner ear, or an inexplicable surfeit of dried skin.

Sometimes as he was gathering notes for his obituary, he would encounter a hitherto unexperienced blankness, a disconcerting silence,

and go to the computer, open the website, and find, in the Lakeside's sheen and grain, an easement.

Sometimes rain on a hillside in Malaysia. Sometimes the dark woodiness of an early-fifties Gibson L-5.

He thought how satisfying it would be to have the coffin inside the house. He wondered what his wife would think, and remembered

when he was young and had suggested to another woman, Eileen, that it might be propitious if her friend Charlotte moved into their apartment.

Dark days brightened slightly by lists: lists of sorrows, lists of obligations. And then suddenly a call, a mix-up at the laboratory: wrong slides, someone else's biopsy.

But still, he had told no one. His was a large house: the coffin would not be too obtrusive if he set it on its end and had a carpenter dado shelves inside,

perhaps it would hold *Stories and Texts for Nothing, Letters of John Keats to His Family and Friends, The Seven Ages,* and *Cemetery Nights.*

XXXVI

Diagnosed, some feel the end, some eat raw broccoli. Brown saw the
    milkman's daughter.

Her hand on his shoulder as a needle plunged to his marrow.

And then every four weeks sat five hours among the turbaned and
    the sleek
in a kind of lounge or discotheque or luxury barge adrift on the
    River Styx.

And this was chemotherapy.

Rituxan dripped. Treanda surged. A Benadryl void. Then the muses
    emerged from the steroids.

Brown's muse was a pianist. Primed.

Stoked. She played a Thorazine scherzo to thwart the hiccups. She was
    his sonata anti-pessimistic.

She was the best time in history to be afflicted.

And the mystery is, she had been there all along,

growing slyly, indolently,
like a crocus or lamb near the crossing where his mother was born.

Shy, dark-skinned, white sundress—in complete remission,
Brown remembers how she climbed on the bus.
And when she got off, that difficulty breathing.

The fear, as now, he might see her again. He was touched and spoken to.

He had not even known she knew his name.

Many dreams fade and darken in the portal. Because Luck retains a full head of hair at sixty and quickens to the bon mot, Marie Spence approaches him to speak to the Lions Club of Greater Cold Springs about her project to gussy up downtown with marigolds and cherry trees. And when she has tempted him with sufficient art to reel him in—"Don't forget: mention the koi pond, the fountain," and "Wear that Hart, Schaffner and Marx blazer," and "Thelonious, lowlights are not just for middle-aged women." When he thinks of public speaking, Luck's hands sweat and his throat constricts, but Mrs. Spence is right: the square has gone to shit. Tar paper on the hardware. Plywood on the depot. On the light pole in front of the closed movie theater the announcements for fire sales, revivals, and tractor pulls have formed a hard, white laminate of papier-mâché. And here he stops, takes out his drawing pad and doodles a cloud under that jubilant word *pentimento*. But the night before the speech, as he sleeps, Luck wakes his wife with a death cry. Not screaming exactly. What do they call it? Ululating. Luck ululates. Then he moans, and it starts again. Snakes in the bath. Men with circles painted under their eyes, jigging spears. When his wife wakes him, he says, "Nothing, I was being eaten." All the following day Luck makes himself remember. To appear calm addressing the cannibals, he will need this fear.

XXXVIII

My birth name is Willard Jackson Tallfeather,
and I found my real parents hidden
in a manila folder in the basement of a courthouse.
Rushing to greet them, twelve
years too late, when I stopped
and said their names, man at the convenience mart

up by the interstate, hawking in a cup,
took off his John Deere cap
and said she had killed him
with a serrated steak knife,
pondered the whole rotten business,
and died of grief. Oil derricks
in the wheat fields near the cemetery
like elephants doing push-ups in dreams.
The trees growing out of their graves
came from China and were sixteen feet tall
with white flowers that did not forgive them.
Though I knew probably she did not mean it.
Torn, she tore him.
And later, like it was a joke he was not in on,
told by the Holy Spirit.
Driving back to Cold Springs, cowboys
who vote for human *T. rex*es
passing in big fucking trucks
on the way to the sale barn
with Tea Party stickers on their bumpers
and shotguns behind their hats—
Luck said once, *The nicest*
people who would ever kill you.
The deer did not see me, blood
filled the wrinkles of my hood. Washing my face
in the restroom of a truck stop outside Branson,
I waited for the wrecker and was Mack again.

XXXIX *(Mack Working on Mann)*

Finally, you must make yourself invisible,
deepening the incision, finding the artery—
desolation inhibitors in your earbuds:
Mix tapes are good, something by Jobim
that says, not him, a mistake, dance;
there are people who look happy dead.
Even with mouths unwired they smile.
Their grayness is not a grayness to fear.
They are not gray like slugs.
They are gray like smoke. They give directions.
Mann was the kind of man who knew
where he came from and where he was going.
Intractable latitudes of face and hands,
chill canvas of the body, art. You do not
revise or sign it, and if you knew him
you brush the teeth before stitching the lips.
Then you must lay him out, destroy nostalgia.

(2012)

54

WAYWARD SWAINS
IN A TIME OF WAR

XL

Nearly inconceivable that Portis served
in the fifth squadron, second platoon
of Company B under the command
of student Sergeant Sizemore, drilling
on the quad, right-facing and left-facing,
about-facing and halting. Every
cadet in green wool, every shoe
spit-shined, every shirt crisply ironed.

Portis his mellowness, Portis the man
of peace, Portis the studmuffin
licking a pistachio ice cream cone
in Kingsport with a girl named Joan,
Portis ever unaudited by the IRS,
Portis live from the Methodist social,

Portis alone in the tub, inventing
a video game called Buenas Noches.

After forty years, a little of the sepia
that alchemizes the neural plaques
and renders humiliation from comedy
makes Portis doubt the specific gravitas,
the mawkish corps d'esprit, and especially
the grounds north of the main stairs
of the library where the shrubbery
gets truly prodigious. Yews, acacias,

rare dwarf species of pyrancantha
and forsythia—student Private Wilson to his right
and student Private Gallo to his left—
Sergeant Sizemore, starting to sweat
the itchy proximities of the front row
to a holly and the rear to a boxwood,
considers suckholes and breech births,
boys on fire and arms flying off.

For soon Colonel Barksdale will arrive
to assess the squad's combat readiness.
This is why the *harch*, *harch*, *harch*
cadence crawls to hiatus. At ease,
Portis, dimly glancing south, regards
the agitprop of the alternate squad
chanting *fuck-fuck-fuck* and *hell-no-I-won't-go*
as they march in mock-step beside them.

A few wear bandages; one crow-hops
on a broken stick; another, dressed

as a cadaver, carries a doll with chest
ripped open to simulate a wound.
On this wound, with its hand-flecked
blood-burst halo, Portis speculates.
On the black dye-job of the Euro-doll,
and the braless funsacks of its bearer.

But the morning stretches long,
the morning arches its back like a cat,
and the colonel strides across the quadrangle.
He has come from West Point and Saigon.
The medals shine heavy on his chest.
When he bristles and snaps one boot
against the other, his eyes lock,
and his *a-ten-hut* reverberates like a slap.

And what is in the colonel's mind?
Imperfect life. Perfect design
that slakes the grace of Archimedes.
With its right flank raised on the sidewalk
and its front row grazing a boxwood,
the squad is of questionable grace. The squad
is an ambulance full of swollen bodies
parked and abandoned by a drunk teenager.

A clusterfuck, a dufus scrum,
a metaphysical reaper with mortal parts,
a crisis for dummies, a test of character.
This is why Portis is made commander,
and gives one order, *Forward, march!*
Oh long ago, useless and irretrievable,

impossible task, battle inside a box —
about Portis, it has been decided.

No more will be required of Portis.
A mistake to have put Portis in charge
in such close quarters with such distractions
as were planted exclusively for men
of exceptional promise and noted
under "Response to Challenge" beside
"Portis is not the kind
of man who dies. Portis gets men killed."

XLI *(Mack, the Breaker)*

Do you see how it was with me?
Skinny and of little account,
then growing abruptly,
my left hand a miasma,
my talent, my vanishing ink,
rubbed into the ball
while fate skulked toward me
in Ho Chi Minh sandals and calico noir?

At fifteen I threw in the high eighties
and two curves:
the slow one broke three feet and took all I had;
the other hard, but easy on the shoulder,
the hand loosening the screw, so the ball
jumped at the plate four inches.

And the jilter, with the whole arm,
but the fingers like a hand

cupped lightly around a breast.
So when the bottom dropped,
the batter stood there
and, for just that instant,
saw his girl opening
as she tiptoed on the top step
of the First Baptist Church
to kiss me.

And now when I slip into the pinstripe
suit of the undertaker, strap
on my hook, and drive downtown
past stores with plywood on the windows
and dried puddles of cement in the back lot of the closed block plant,
I think of things like black holes
and time machines that will never happen.

Though I know it was only a pitch,
there and then not, here
each night it breaks
when I touch and am touched,
where I hold and am held,
and, in sleep, run through the jungle by the light of tracers,
dive, and as I dive,
yank the pin and toss the grenade
into the dark hut. Onliness

of a nanosecond, then cut—
the batter and the burning people can keep their guilt.
I could not help my greatness.
I was courted early, recruited
from far away.

Three doctors have prescribed two pills,
so I may speak softly to the widow,
choose the songs, arrange the service,
and late in the afternoon
when the mourners have left,
direct the backhoe operator
to drop the dark shovel-loads
of loam onto a new grave.

But always like a woman's eye finds me—
where each point of my life
makes contact with every other,
I raise my head
from between her legs
and see her looking back at me.

I owe the dead everything
and am happy. Days when no one dies
I drive my Cadillac out the Corn Road,
park at the gate of the old
African Methodist cemetery,
tombstones like sheep. Everything
perfect, the tree and the little hill.
If there is a God, I believe
there will be cemeteries in heaven.
                              But later,
as I fill the tank, old man at the next pump says,
"Only you could've hit your own breaker,"
and I see myself like I am still,
waiting for myself, but also thrown

and throwing, the mound
where I will always be confident.

The itch in the ring finger of my missing hand
is evidence of the time I was fooled
in a market outside Quang Tri —
a little girl offered me a fruit,
then the hand flies up as though for a question,
the mangoes scatter from the stalls,
the hearing goes out of my left ear,
and the letters from the Dodgers stop.

XLII

Brown the ed-psych man staring at a plaster wall of paisley doves
as he applies the theories of Skinner to a model fifth-grade class
and blows a plexi-sauna of homegrown marijuana;

Mann in a brown study, legging up for the space race
by gnawing toothmarks down his slide rule
as he mumbles over the text of Quantitative Analysis.

Well, it is not going well — in sum, it feels like hell —
and friend-gossip is the valve when things do not go well.

Mann complains to Portis: once
when they tripped, Brown lay all night observing the ceiling, cooing,
"Frog syndicate" and "Magellanic clouds."

Brown tells Mills of these selfsame hours:
Mann pacing with incarnadine face, then vanishing
until they went and found him shaking his fist at a light,
shouting, "Change, you motherfucker, change!"

Not ideal companions, to say the least. No,
Portis tells Mills: Mann is a date thief:

that business in the closet: Mann with Brown's sweetie:
her pale thong whitecapping among his penny loafers.

Mills cites other occasions:

Mann with his own honey; Brown across the room
demonstrating blood-pressure adjustment from his bed: "Imagine,
let's say, you're holding a live grenade, now suck
your asshole through the top of your head";

Mann after the Warhol lecture, resplendent in blond wig,
slit skirt, and pearls, lip-synching "Fever." The same
night Brown saw it was Millicent, it had always been Millicent,
the Methodist minister's daughter, whom he truly loved.
A call, an afternoon, weekend visits from Cold Springs.
Mann's second cousin: *this settles things.*

Except one night before a party, a joint —
she's never tried it.
It pleases them she wants to take a hit:

itsy tokes, then bigger,
until, comatose on the sofa, at peace,
she sits up like a spring.
"I'm blind," she says,
"I can't see a friggin' thing."

This instant then
as Brown bolts for the healing kitty —
Mann whispers, "George,
we shall have to kill her."

XLIII

At Queen City and Ninth on Friday night driving east,
Mills caught in a flash at the corner of his eye
a black limousine closing fast
at a perpendicular and headed
straight through him.

No honk, no scream. He checked
both sides, ahead, behind. Intact. Still there
mailboxes, houses, yards his headlights fixed,
smoothed over and glided past,
and friends in the back seat, unbroken,
unimpaled, and not noticing
anything auspicious.

But ever afterward Mills was dead. Things hollowed;
women walked past him and did not speak—
of course, he only constructs this afterlife
that's now and here and does not weigh a thing.
Not like he's fundamentalist.

More like the tense of being here relaxed
and Mills sprang free. The limousine
went south and he to a party
where things undone meet things unsaid and make no noise,
ask no questions.

A cool night, mid-November, leaves not falling yet—
The soul, when first released
from mutability, gathers its bearings.
When you're dead, it's hard to say what else is dead,

but for Mills death was not a vision of things.
Death was absolute clarity.

XLIV

To read *The Waste Land* at thirteen, to solve the problem
second in Algebra II or Trigonometry and shrink
from the blackboard in disgust;
first in Literature, first in History, first
to ascend the bare breast-on-breast
French kiss, man-up to the biological prerogative
and become papa:
was this your story, Lonely Luck?

To register for junior college and enlist in the National Guard,
to have a mother-in-law. Matron-styled but
girlish at thirty-one: with her long hair bunned
in a red kerchief, she seemed ripe
for the three spot
in the traditional
five-generation photograph.

Sundays, flashing his diamond rings,
your father-in-law,
a construction-boss-Germanophile atheist,
held forth
on Nietzsche and Heidegger
from his La-Z-Boy recliner.

To choose without thought *her* loveliness over a career.

Walking before dinner from up the big house,
past gamecocks, donkey, and pet skunk
to the hill of goats, seeing all things
caricatured, thinking, *None of it,*
none of it is real. You shout
and the goats faint.

(1967–1971)

THE RIGHTEOUS TRIP

XLV

Nine months and fifty-seven hits of acid, Portis.
Makes lucidity appealing. Stop. No
visions cling, but starlings alighting
in a tree have things to say to him.

Often when he shuts his eyes, he sees
the white sole of a foot adrift in space.
If he focuses on this foot, the flesh
undulates, and in the waves, an eye appears.

Elevators, escalators, brown liquor, Mack.
Mack back from Nam, his missing hand like a bride
who has gone to powder her nose
in a filling station restroom and will not return.

Ludes. Crystal in great-grandmotherland.
Adjustment period. Blue nights scratched

on white mornings, suicide notes
half written, unmeant, and unaddressed.

Why are they hitching west? Portis
has an Incomplete and must write
the final paper for religion class.
In an oft-recurring dream Portis searches

for the saloon where this class meets.
The title of the paper is "How Long
Can a Person Live in America
on Goodwill and Seventeen Dollars?"

XLVI

The road winds through hickories
by truck patches under bluffs. Stop.
A mountain picks them up. The mountain
says, "Cut your goddamned hair."

Mack fresh meat in Freak 101, his Purple Heart set
on silent rant, his man-doll prosthesis
flung in the slough behind the block plant.
Portis dean-smacked, on furlough as a scholar.

Mack studies the stump.
The stump as it heals has taken on
the glossy tints of a bottle tree
or stained-glass window.

Through the glass, people Mack has killed:
a girl with half a face, a man on fire.
These haints speak to him.
He does not speak of them.

Slow hitching, Muscle Shoals to Memphis.
Cotton rows, cows. Something Mrs.
Mack said before they left:
"Seth, find out why Cedric is the way he is."

XLVII

North of Memphis, when he starts to ask,
Mack's right thumb is like a tongue saying stop.
Big fellow in a big Plymouth pulls over:
tattoos, black hair slicked down.

Jet engine mechanic, drives fast.
A doer, not a talker. No problem.
The big Plymouth sails and seems to shear the delta
until he lets them out, Little Appleton, pop. 43.

A church, a school, a feed store, a few houses
softly coming on, the fields before them
like pretty women in romantic novels
saying, "Don't hurt me, Lance, be gentle."

XLVIII

Twilight riding with a very white man
in a light blue seersucker suit

and light blue Cadillac with letters on the door
of the local gospel station.

Mack in the front with gladsome song,
Portis in the back, juicy
from the ministrations of Elijah,
the big black poodle.

This preacher driving slowly through the hills
like Mrs. Zora Neatsfoot on Decoration Day
after her stroke, haltingly quoting
the hundredth psalm.

This preacher drives very very slowly,
from Little Appleton to the center
of St. Louis. "Why were we put here on this earth?"
he asks before he lets them off.

XLIX

The black BMW brakes, idles as they run up to it,
rolls forward, and backs up again. Stop.
Neil Shapiro, home from Brandeis,
cruising, nothing else on the platter, Friday night

his mother's car, some aleatory chatter
before questions. For Portis: "Do you read Schopenhauer?"
For Mack: "Got any weed?"
To see Mack roll a joint on his stump

is to feel a craft like panic. Shapiro
wows, drags bottom, coughs, tunes in

Country Joe and the Fish.
Slows down, speeds up, slows down,

pulls onto the shoulder at St. Joseph,
opens the door to let them out,
thinks again, says "What the fuck, get back in,"
and talks Plato all the way to Columbia.

L

When men grow long hair in 1973
it is a symbol with many dimensions
for one thing their unconcern
they will be snatched up into machines

for another a metamorphosis
of the superego a lightness
like breathing after a long forced run
deep into the territory of women

a stimulus to cast off belts
and sport dashikis this period
in American history is limited
when young white men embrace

their blackness and stroll
through parks of large cities
sans underwear the breeze up
their pants hirsute freedom

that makes them believe
for this small hiatus in history

they are exhaling not inhaling
they are not dicks but teats

ante-Watergate demi-hippies
with pencil ponytails one dip
of the Dow hair goes south
stop the men are dicks again

slumped at urinals they trickle
they know soon they must
find work to find work
they will have to pee in a cup

LI

Almost two hours Portis and Mann wait. Then cold
and hungry shuffle up the ramp
to a filling station for two 35-cent
incorporeally dry approximately

pimento cheese sandwiches
from a vending machine and go back down through rain and cuss
their eighth-grade shop teacher
and Richard Nixon and discuss the project of the moneyless life.

One thing Portis had thought of and forgot:
to bring fishing line and hooks
to catch ducks in municipal parks.
"Or we might," says Mack, "hypnotize chickens."

LII

The night shines in the portal of the years.
The night beside the freeway grows
whiskers, then a Volkswagen bus, sunrise
panels: "What's happening?" and they're in

as far as Kansas: the night miles
out there through the nimbus.
Next the city,
a duplex near the center:

three kinds of granola in jars high
on shelves secured by concrete blocks;
the shock of ammonia rising from the kitty litter.
It is a moment of high resolution

and vision, no names have been exchanged.
A woman in braids walks from room to room,
like consciousness itself, looks under things,
and, scurrying to the door, screams

the cat's name, "*Cedric!*" and after
a while, in runs the vagrant kitty.
No sweat, but Mack is white as Christmas,
and Portis sees him dangling on a string.

LIII

Short rides question or make claims.
"Why do you live the way you do?"

"What do your parents think?"
"What is it really like, being in an orgy?"

"Do you consider this journey a vision quest?"
In trucks the country takes off its mask.
Kansas nodding off, a dream of elms.
Once Mack wakes with a hand in his lap.

Friendly said he was called to be a cowboy.
Near Colorado the same plains,
but rougher claims and tougher questions:
"Oh, us? Haw-haw, we're going to fuck a squaw."

"You say you read philosophy, boy.
Ever hear the one about the tree falling
in the woods when no one's there?
Does it make a sound? I was there. It didn't."

LIV

Time and they sleep in the Hebrides
atop an incline under an overpass
and do not hear the silence grow
when trucks stop passing

and wake and know then it is snow.
The blizzard asks, "How long
can a person live in America
on goodwill and seventeen dollars?"

And though they had never been,
in childhood, close, they cleave

now one to the other. Sleep.
In Cold Springs roosters crow,
but wind's zambonied a slick of ice
on the incline. They fester in a trap.

LV

All morning white of death,
white of cousin skin.
The sky lifts and mottles.
The sky is a dead man's stomach.

The second night, Portis talks
of crossing the causeway to Key West,
though he has only read of this himself,
and Mack smiles and looks

for purchase where they can leap across the ice.
Then Portis sees: asleep,
Mack does not dream.
Death thoughts make him calm.

LVI *(The One-Legged Deputy Sheriff of Thomas County)*

Sunlight takes. They wait. They leap,
and after an eight-mile trudge through snow,
their plan to barter sweeping for a bed
dies in the mouth of the hotel clerk.

The deputy comes in an unmarked van.
A sniper once, who tripped a mine,

the deputy walks on hobnail boots.
He shoves them in the back and holds his nose.

The cell stinks: lidless john, two cots.
On one, a loose deck of cards.
Stale joke: some drunk has ripped
the lower face from the jack of clubs.

Tin plate of powdered eggs, skunk coffee.
The meantime trance hardly sleep
before it's interrupted. Fluorescent
light, four officers: three big men,

happy with themselves; one runt
with Bowie knife. Howdy, Mr. Dillon.
Time to fumigate, trim those dainty curls.
When the deputy laughs, a cobra

coils in Mack; his nub strikes
above his eyebrow, a crisp salute,
Reporting for duty! The deputy's look
before Mack's deep We are grateful, sir!

LVII

Always charity drives. It does not ride.
Night turns to day and day to night
and they can scarcely believe
it's dark: a Hindu minute ago,

let out by the Boulder police station,
they walked an hour aimlessly,

then, hungry, panhandled quarters
for two 89-cent spaghetti platters.

But it is two weeks. They sleep
on borrowed mats. Neither cleans
nor cooks. The resident swami
who loaned Portis *Slaughterhouse-Five*

and *Fear and Trembling* quits
inveigling him to join the commune.
The English major from Portland,
who cried out in Mack's arms,

washed his shirts, and called him
Soul Brother, slams the door
and brandishes her flag, a pair
of passion killers on a broom.

LVIII

Man named Boris with an ad
in the window: *Chess Games,
twelve players, twenty-second
move limit. Entry Fee: $100.*

Mack and Portis sit down
across from two half-winsome
convert disciples
of Chögyam Trungpa Rinpoche.

They are quiet as temple rats.
Sometimes when one leaves

for yoga, the other backslides
and reads Mack's palm.

Once the artist sketched them—
not Mack and Portis, the Buddhists.
He made them mermaids.
Mack and Portis meditate.

They do not know they meditate
until it's habit.
One day the artist drives them
through icy aspens to his cabin.

One day the chess master
tells them of Odessa.
It is all one thing after a while.
They compare friends far off.

The artist talks *Kama Sutra*
to the shy Baptist waitress
the way he looks at aspens
while painting the ocean.

LIX

They will not speak of this again:
the question Who are you
among the repetitions of poverty,
then silence, then motherfucker;

never say who first said shut up
or which swung wildly,

or whether either saw blood
and recalled in exhaustion a lesson.

An embarrassment of violence,
a tumble down a slope, they embrace
in a choke hold. The Zen stallion.
The good Nazi at Nuremberg.

Noon a week finds them riding east.
Snowy ridges. Portly salesman
—THINK POSITIVE button—
wondering what's in their bags.

They travel with this present
from a lawyer's daughter:
six perfect buds in a basket
woven of leaves and stems.

                LX

In a warren of south-seeking
ladies looking down from windows—
the ladies have this horror
at the indecency of breeches.

Men lost together
have a silent moulding
and influencing power
over each other.

They interassimilate. This
is the world. They cannot

expect to give many hours away
to pleasure. They walk

confidently, for
they do not think of walking,
though Mack knows by darting,
sidereal glances

he is black with a capital B, and Portis
walks as in a book with no index
or table of contents,
feels the light rain, and thinks

of John Keats in Scotland
waking in a smoky house
one hundred fifty years ago
with a scalding throat.

L X I

Mann's apartment in Denver is manly,
immaculate, tasteless. The windows
behind the blinds look out on walls.
Mann works for a mine reclamation company.

The walls inside are lists of duties.
Drive to Yellowwood. Test the creek.
The refrigerator brims with champagne.
The champagne opens the portal.

Balloons in this part of the portal.
Jawaharlal Mills's sixth birthday.

He climbs a tree and breaks his arm.
Why do men laugh at pain? Vanquished,

it pours the vantage of its absence.
It makes a comfortable reunion theme.
Mack pops another cork. The portal
shifts. Mills's twenty-first,

the night he claims he is dead.
In this, Portis observes the trinity:
Mack is the Savior; Mann, God the father;
and Mills, the Holy Spirit

because he sees farther than most.
Mann worries on Mills. What
is he studying out there in Palo Alto?
The quark, says Portis. The quark?

asks Mann. Yes, the quark,
and inside the quark, a woman's shoe.
Thirteen and a half, triple-E.
And that was the first day.

LXII

The second day Mann drives them to Pikes Peak,
a new black Mustang, faux-fur steering wheel.
They go up clouds past the tree line.
The wind carves pockets of clarity.

But at the top, when they get out,
the cold bites; the distances beneath,

the towns and ranches, draw a curtain.
This is a view they will always imagine.

The third day, Mann stocks the fridge.
Pickles, pork cutlets, milk, and beer.
The fourth, he returns to engineering.
On their own, Portis and Mack find a gym.

Bored after work, Mann takes them to the bars
only he would take them to. The Line,
with women in checks and men in string ties.
The Golden Bull, where elk heads line the walls.

At Girls' Town, the mayor takes Mann's hand,
freshens it on her nipples, then leads them
to a table near the stage. Big Mann,
says Mack. Licks his finger, and raises a one.

LXIII

Thursday, when Mann is busy they take the car,
drive south until the houses get small and dark,
and stop at a neon sign, *The Buzzard Mechanic*.
A man named Buddy Blue Eagle buys them shots.

His woman is Bleeding Dog. She sings.
When they go out to his truck, he reaches
in the glove compartment: a big stash,
mostly buds, held down by a Colt revolver.

Cheyenne stone. Cheyenne logic.
Spirit lodge, dream charm, Sand Ridge.

The Dairy Queen in Laramie has the best hot dogs.
Bleeding Dog has a PhD in Comparative Literature.

And time in time will double, vintage,
Scratched, sparked by a passing lighter.
What is so funny about now, and the moon,
cowboy-faced, spurring its dark horse?

Portis goes alone into the portal. The foot
floats out of space, waves ripple in the sole,
and when the eye appears, he sees
the eye is the eye of Reba, his mother.

But, behind the eye, the foot changes
to a mountain, and when he looks closer
it has changed to the eye of providence
on the back of the dollar bill.

LXIV *(An Insignificant Accident Occurs)*

between thoughts on a laughing question after a turn—
three bumps, and the Mustang
breaches on a stairway
that descends into a tunnel.

How quickly, yet already they're doing better.
Mack expresses this very opinion
as they crawl through the back seat
and out the window. Lucky,

agrees Portis, and soon four men appear.
A simple task: five lift, one rocks—

a jiffy and they're free: at home, they check:
no serious damage, one trifling mark.

A lover's scratch, hardly worth mentioning.
On the ninth night, Mann serves filet mignon.
Just help yourself, he says, when I'm not here.
Morning comes up easy. The day is flat.

He drives to work. They walk to gym.
Archived in a journal: warm morning,
tenth day of visit, $8.27. No visions now.
On the eleventh day, the fridge is empty.

(1973)

BOOK TWO

PUBERTY IN COLD SPRINGS

LXV

Clean world of the twilight field as the lights come on.
The grass freshly mown, the base paths dragged

and spritzed. Sounds of fungoes popping flies. Clean
snaps of grounders against gloves. Pitchers warming

up. Thunks and thuds of fastballs, arcs of Cedric Mack's
curves. Clean world, dry county. But the man named

Moon, who will announce the action from the booth
above the concession stand, is high on Dexedrine,

and the man named Cloud prays for sportsmanship
and good, fair competition with malt liquor on his breath.

Planed smooth by auctions and benefit dinners, the field
is like the night. The storm that two hours ago turned

the sky black and green has passed east. Cars parked
by the fence purr like bobcats drinking from a ditch.

Fathers on the hoods hoot and laugh. Bleacher mothers
blossom in the colors of their affiliations. The youngest

hold infants. The oldest puff menthol cigarettes and carry
smut books in straw bags. Every boy on the field is an all-star

and pitched for his local team, but here likeness ends.
Except for brothers and cousins, no two players

from Cold Springs resemble each other. The batboy
was a blue baby. The second baseman throws

with two good fingers and a nub. Tarrant City players
appear older and drawn from a larger pool. Several

already sprout mustaches or goatees. The one who
resembles a young Karl Marx hides in his gym bag

a picture of a topless starlet. In six years he will die
half a world away in a bamboo grove, the same

picture in his pocket. If you said later, this was the year
of the Bay of Pigs, three months after the Freedom

Riders, someone would add, *Mack Mack pitched four
no-hitters. Dudley Mann set a record with eleven*

home runs. Chalmers hit .721. The prime distinction
between the people of the world— talent— matters here

more than any other distinction. And still some rumor
about the dark-complected pitcher springs up

on the Tarrant City side, and runs south and eddies
in stare-downs and whisper fights. Until the Negro

question is duly asked, and settled with birth certificate,
barbecue plates, introductions to mama, and "Heavens

no." Before the chants start, as always, "Mack Mack.
Mack Mack. Mack Mack." Before the umpire dusts

off the plate, rolls his wheelchair behind the catcher,
clicks the counter in his fist, and calls "Play ball."

LXVI *(The Age of Accountability)*

Question for Protestants: did one reach it at puberty,
or, by some fluke of preternatural maturity
or wit, could some arrive earlier,
say, ten or eleven, when rogue prodigals
were already scratching starter fires,
ripping nudes from encyclopedias,
or shifting blame when change went missing?

Twelve, most seemed to agree, the big bang
of boobs, legs, compacts, condoms, and mascara
when girls, with parental permission, might
cross the state line to Georgia and marry.
Though of course no specific age was given,
like sixteen to drive or fifteen for a learner's permit;
the age of eligibility for eternal perdition was ambiguous.

Thus these long discussions, in shallow water
as afternoon sun clipped the edge of the quarry,

of sixteen-year-old boys and eleven-year-old women —
Seth Portis said Catholics were covered from birth.
Jews had bar mitzvahs, and idiots were flame-proof.
But Bobby James Chalmers demurred. No Catholics.
No Jews. No idiots. A person had to be born again.

And this was easy: you went up front at altar call.
It helped to cry, but you did not have to cry.
You kneeled, you said some words, and you were in.
But first, baptism! No dice if you died before
baptism, there was scripture on this: children
on fire, and babies and morons, too, burning forever.

And you had to be wholly immersed, not sprinkled —
how radiantly imbecilic this struck Jawaharlal Mills,
but he studied more the muscles in the shoulders
as Chalmers dived back in and swam toward the deep end
and this image would linger after the pastor yanked
him from the pew, read two verses from Leviticus,
dabbed neatsfoot oil above one eye, and cast out the demon.

LXVII

Year of the change, year of the dragon,
Brown slept through numbers,
slept through words, woke
on the bus, a beatnik,
bopped to the house,
hands lifted to chest, limp-
wristed like Maynard G. Krebs,
and read the *Cold Springs Daily*.

Bull Connor, George
Wallace, Medgar Evers.
Dark days settling
with the light. One night
he grew nine inches
and the next day announced
in Civics class,
"I am a communist."

His face broke out,
his set shot grew a jump shot.
His Pet of the Month was a dream
of marching with King.
Standing at the foul line,
he dribbled four times. His
nickname echoed back:

COACH IS HOT
PLAYERS COOLER
SINK IT SINK IT MARTIN LUTHER.

Crunch-time stream of puberty drama:
Brown: "I will ask Jamequa Hodge to the hop."
The ball rolling on the rim: yes or no?

The young crow
with broken wing
he found under the pear tree —
raised in a box,
fed to health,

and named Zachariah
(because it was black)—

flew off to be with other crows
sometimes, came back, shat
on Brown's head, and
did not appear
to love him.

LXVIII *(Mrs. Lionel Spence at Fifteen)*

There are girls who must speak to trees
after dreams they don't cleanly remember.
Sometimes they remember water.
That was why she woke wet and thought
there had been a wave, then a man, and nothing
like this had ever happened, with no
volition, but the wave lingered,
as though it had taken him whole
and swallowed him with her hips.

She thought, *Am I an awful person?*
and washed her panties in the sink.
The tree she spoke to was a pin
oak. It was some kind of blind psychic
or priest who'd outstripped religion,
but also old, not fond
of trivia, so she chanted and improvised.
O tree, she would begin each time,
and lay her coat down at her feet.

Some days light rain, sometimes just breeze—
she chanted *moss, lightning, wind,*
and it never varied, this tryst
with the silent tree, though she knew
no limb could tell another limb.
Just once she thought to say this wave,
this nerve she had touched and now
must touch again, was good, but kept
this to herself. Even a tree might get ideas.

LXIX

The day Portis was assigned
the free paper, he saw
three things that interested him:
a hawk carrying a snake,
a letter John Keats wrote
to John Hamilton Reynolds
from Scotland in 1818,
and a woman in
the outhouse behind the church,
peeing standing up.

Then he went as ordered
by his grandmother
to help collect rent
from the Ledbetters
and waited with
his granddaddy
on the porch. A long time.

A pig ran out the door
and soon three chickens.
A wasp got after him,
and all the time,
the smell from inside
made a racket. *Cat,*
thought Portis,
not pig or chicken,
and sure enough,
out sauntered a little
towheaded girl dragging
a kitty by its ears.

Then the old lady, Rosellen,
who always got
his grandaddy's goat,
emerged, studied him
a piece, tousled
the young'un's hair, and said,
"Annky, thay oddam."
And when it didn't bite,
paused and cackled,
then said it again,
"Annky, thay oddam."

"Mizz Ledbetter,"
said granddaddy,
"if you'll be
so polite as to get shed
of that snuff,
I'll try and consider

precisely
what you're meaning."

And then she did, she
spat, if spitting
is not a pit or coop,
but a cathedral: a swallow
that gathered an insweep
to a cleansing hawk
that squeaked the springs
and set the red wad
flying between them
to resolve against
a rusty sheet of tin.

Whereon Mrs. Ledbetter repeated,
but this time cleaner,
"Nancy," and rubbed
the little girl's towhead,
"say goddam for these
nice gentymen." And when
the little girl complied,
the old lady smiled,
winked at Portis's granddaddy,
raised her dress,
blew her nose on the hem,
and cackled again.

A funny thing
occurred to Portis then,
with darkness over it,

the madness of an old man
and old woman who
might have kissed long
ago at a Christmas
party under mistletoe,
and maybe it went further.

In any event, there would be no rent,
there never was, and
grandma Portis didn't like it.
And mumbled as she fried
their tongue. Then sat a spell
in solitary, and dragged
a ball and chain of silence
to the organ and pumped on
"Softly and Tenderly, Jesus Is Calling"
for a little more than an hour.
Then was restored herself again.

But back to the paper
Portis had intended to write.
In bed, he thought about it,
and two parts stirred:
not the hawk and snake
D. H. Lawrence might handle;
or Keats's letter,
which sounded like Mark Twain;
or what occult ecclesiastical
hygiene might warrant
a Christian woman peeing standing up.

More, what was meant by free?
And if he was, he felt
the spiders in those marks he hated,
which hung there in the air,
stung what people said,
and spun the web around it.
And felt the secret labor
press upon the paper.

A rainy night. He was alone.
And tried on words like shirts.
And scratched the loneliness of the burden.

Then went down to the kitchen
to make himself some coffee
and saw the words
all shining in the cupboard.
Some waited for company
that never came. Mainly
these stayed clean.
But others rattled against ice
and woke him late at night.
This was the goddam South.
Some words
he'd need to put
in other people's mouths.

LXX

These three seventh-graders giggling down the hall of Cold Springs Junior High School, leaning on one another and whispering into each other's ears, resemble three willows that ascend from a single trunk. They keep one diary. One bird darts among them on the stealthy, half-nervous tremor of the worry that next year will come breasts and boys, but now they radiate a sanguine health, a preternatural closeness. Their teacher does not know them well, but she marks their shyness and exclusive rectitude, their light canopy and banter. One rustle when they settle in adjacent desks; one motion when they turn to the sun in the west window. For part of one more year, they will sway together as ungainly trunks and limbs. And then, a little eyeliner, a dab of lipstick; just so, no willow remains a willow forever. Already the tall one in the dark green sweater tears up and does not applaud with her classmates when the principal announces that John Fitzgerald Kennedy, the thirty-fifth president of the United States, has been shot in Dallas. She raises her head slightly. She looks to each side. But her friends, celebrating the downfall of the Antichrist, have not yet seen her. There is just the one moment before the second announcement: she could smile and save face; for all her shyness, she could say *Ringo;* she could even dance—she knows the Twist, the Watusi, and the Mashed Potato; but she is hit hard. Proud and angry, she is split to the root.

LXXI

Hope came and surrounded
the trailer behind the sawmill
with cars and men with guns,
whereon the megaphone police
began as he'd been taught

to speak on dire occasions
—gently and with sweet reason—
to heal the hurt inside the trailer
lay down the rifle come out
and let them go the minutes then
you think you're in a corner
but you're not and love and Jesus
two little cottonhead boys
and the girl still in diapers
no matter what you think Letitia's done
and then his mother came she said
you always been a good boy Bruce
and Brother Latham too
after six hours a bald coach
a favorite cousin told a joke
until the husband said *Letitia*
bring the children to the door
one by one and give them out
to your mama but him eighteen
pilled-up drunk the light
no matter what would happen
was starting in the east
like a diesel in January
everyone crying to stay calm the beacon
still coming on going off
in the tower on the mountain.

LXXII *(Reba's Fastidium)*

No dirt on her floor, no smudge on her windows,
Bone china immaculate in maple cabinet,
No germs on the glass knobs, no fleck or mote
On the counters, her house a prophylactic
Against the imperfectability of the world.

She sweeps, she dusts, she sees the problem,
Rips the needlepoint aphorism, then starts again.
She does not say *shit*. She does not even spell it.
So her daughter will not holler like a Holy Roller
Or belch and expectorate like a hillbilly.

And each morning she looks into her mouth,
Her ears, she spits the cowlick flat,
She straightens the bangs, she smoothes the hem.
If she sees a thing that brays, she kills it.
And the daughter sees the fate tax, the God question.

With mother eyes she toted
Like a satchel up the steps of the school bus
And will drag to the ventilator,
She sees the unspeakable Protestant mortal sins:
Smoking, drinking, fucking.

Like sandwiches not cut into triangles
Or packed under the calico cloth,
As if a picnic were not a picnic
Unless carried in a lined basket,
As if sin were not harm but bad taste,

And these eyes never leave the daughter
Simply in or outside herself
(If her soul were a coat, these eyes would be buttons)—
The good eye loving, the bad eye scarred
By (she thought she heard) romantic fever.

Apparently this condition is irreversible
Though she does fine. She excels. It is an instinct
After all for the mother to love her baby
And the nurse lays Elizabeth on her belly
Like an outboard motor on a table.

LXXIII

Why is Luck so reverb and chill,
exempted from Sunday school,
allowed to dye his hair green,
and given extra time in the portal
to noodle and tweak the aria
of his pastoral opera buffa,
Norman, Boy of the Woods?

With Mann on bass and Portis on drums,
when he first performs it
live from the screen porch
across from the tent revival
as the esteemed visitor,
the oil baroness, Sister Hunt,
launches her testimony
on the perks of the second birth,

he cranks the amp to ten,
sings falsetto like a castrato,
and makes his telly scream.

Now he reverberates through beauty shops.
Now even barbers are beginning to leak.

Sixteen, silk, an inch better than six feet,
he is dog handsome and sui generis.
But refuses to play any game with balls.
Has declared a ban on casseroles.
Loves cartoons more than the Holy Spirit.
The windows in his portal fog.
His soul is petrichor. Everything
but breasts disappoints him.

In Algebra II he has been caught
drawing a globe with two nipples.
"Mr. Luck," the teacher says when he
finds him doodling nude kangaroos
in the margins of Vocational Ag
after sneaking peeks at Thomas Hardy,
"your heads are too large for your bodies."

(1950, 1961–1967)

DID YOU SEE ANY
OF THE OTHERS
WHILE YOU WERE THERE

LXXIV *(Elegy for the Crooked and Out of the Way)*

They paved the Corn Road, straightened curves
around shade trees, constructed bridges over fords —
paved smokehouse mimosas, burial mounds, and words —
a coarseness and rigidity, a tightness along fence lines.

Some was dead set clear against it. Others kept their own counsel.

Paved hills where mares shied and panthers crossed,
blue stones wheelrowing to the verges, shape notes
flung sideways in the rearview of the rented tour bus
of the Preservation Music Club of St. Louis. Stop.
Transpose key for the blind girl. Blacktop
to halt horse-drawn wagons and suicidal car-chasing dogs.

Everything suspended, everything quoted and framed.

Road of boredom wishes, road to the singing ice-cream social,
road like a read curl shaved from the cedar of a coffin.

Dead battery for snakes, for turtles, dust-talcumed in dog days
or washed out in late April to the corrugation of bedrock.

An advantage for everybody, a travesty they voted to pave it.

That retention of curves for shade trees. Paved.
Like a pear tree in cotton. Paved the aggravation
a woman took to dig up the plow, and walk
the mule around it: worth cider and preserves
preserved in the rockers outside the Cracker Barrel.

Anyway I'd go to Walmart, Walmart or the co-op,
if I was looking for post-hole diggers or bib overalls.

Paved the well digger's daughter who fried whatever
her boys trapped or shot: muskrats, mockingbirds
(you can't hardly go anywhere you can get terrapin anymore).

That man bred mice for medical experiments. Sweet.
That Walmart greeter met Sam Walton. Just like you and me.
That man graduated from Columbia with a degree in Classics.
Kept a junk store, cited Lucretius. Lord Amighty, he could cuss.

Paved there is just no telling why that one-eyed woman
stirring the big black vat of cracklings after the hog slaughter
could not stop talking of Cristóbal Balenciaga and Coco Chanel.

That woman, Una Mae, *unnamed* on the birth certificate.

That gal was in the pen awhile. Said she'd rather kill men than dogs.
The one whose daddy shot the boy for throwing back that fish.
Said he knew the world was ending when he went to the store
and shit fire they was actually selling shit for $2 a bag.

Paved well houses and storm pits. It is all
a right smart different now. Nobody knows who all.
Used to know everybody from Salem to Fountain Bluff. Know
one neighbor now, quiet fellow, a crop duster, and he is moving.

Paved the bootlegger lived on a foothill of a larger
wooded foothill people conceived of as a mountain,
school just to the west, consolidated and emended
to the road-grader driver's house (two daughters: cute,

intelligent; one son: ducktailed, talentless, anticipating
stardom. His signature fading riff and Brutus kiss:
"I will remember you when I'm famous"). Stop.

Paved the school's limed privy hole, from which once,
a dim son, besmeared with fecal slime and crying
in rage and mortification, clambered up a lowered rake
into a life in which he was called to proclaim
the gospel of Jesus Christ, who would regularly appear

on a throne of white light outside his bedroom window
and instruct him as to the proper length of skirts,
what jewelry was permissible, and how Christians should vote.

That place where the boy drowned on a dare was the sump.

That place was called Buzzard's Roost. That hole
up by the bluffs went down forever. They called it the Tangling Hole.
That place called Blowing Springs — the Cherokee
stopped, made camp, and slaughtered a steer, leaving nothing,

no bone hook, shred of tendon, or flake of flint. That woman
made a living painting pumpkinseeds. That man,
born on the isle of Crete, worked as a cotton picker
and was relieved three mornings a week
to teach his master's children Greek.

LXXV

The big fucking truck where you can drive
miles without seeing a soul does not seem
unseemly especially if you have a few
head of Black Angus to haul to market
or bags of guano to load and unload

Neither should one assume these men
abuse their ewes or prioritize universal
nuclear armament if a few prefer
hunting hand-fed lions named Boo or Shorty
to an evening at the philharmonic

Mack smokes with them and hayed in their barns
before W's pet wars when lofts still meant
stings and rectangular bales He has replaced
a rear engine seal and got it wrong
He has held his nose and sold a lemon

The cult of the big truck is waning sad
as any lapsed permission the cab's dumb jokes
the big man's crude "Big tool need big shed"
and the prude's "f-u-c-k"-saffron-sprinkle in a dish
where free dumping's big as Jesus and sneering past a Prius

Mack thinks of gentler people but must they clump
in cities like newsprint blown against a post
that bears a guiding light or commute at five
to palatial suburban digs to feel what's near
and ticking like bay oysters in thermostats

Frogs fields fertilities decisions that never
obtain without some deal chucking a puddle
of glacier to the drills The big fucking truck
is never green Out here Mack waves as it roars past
and buries these people and also drives or rides

LXXVI

The first Alabamian to solve for n at thirteen without knowing y,
Jawaharlal Mills learns at twenty-seven of the hundreds who
did so knowing.

And feels, with sudden Boolean completeness,
his Erdös number ascend and vanish. Riding

his bike in the Palo Alto hills, he is an untouchable hillbilly Houdini.

He gives over his work with the quark.
His adviser advises cybernetics.

In the moments before sleep he goes fractal and envisions
in the sky over the Golden Gate his fortune:
a string of code he will purloin from Atari

to splice into the software of Wang, Lester, and Lovingood
like a porcine valve in the human heart.

And takes heart that at least he is not a doctor.
The summer boys in the baths on Castro.

One day, a truck in his lane, he veers and breaks his arm.

On Demerol he dreams Albert Einstein
into a Jewish Mark Twain, emerges
from the steam, sits down beside him, and whispers "Y'all."

LXXVII

Shroud of Turin morning. Shrubs
emerge from fog like soldiers
limping out of battlefields.
Coffee and the news go down.
Stretched out in rows on truck beds,
the dead are silver; the dead
are like perfect lines of blow.
And now Mack dons old clothes
and finds the right wrench hidden.
The compartment under the sink
is four feet wide, three feet deep,
raised two inches from the tile.
Aridity of dead spiders. Plastic
coils running from cold and hot
water lines to the central spigot.
This is like trees on long walks,
getting around or breaking past
scrums of abrasives, two plungers,
host of rags and rubber gloves.

This is the work of forgetting.
Back hard on edge, flashlight in teeth,
Mack works alone. No second opinion.
The smell more than anything,
a root canal, a dead friend's socks.
Every night the dead stop here.
The goop in the trap is black and green
and holds the hair of children.
For an instant he rolls them
on his stump and shuts their eyes,
then pushes them into the river.

FACEBOOK POST
THURSDAY, 11:56 P.M.
SEPTEMBER 14, 2014

CANDACE D. LARRIMORE

Please help get the word out to all dove hunters in the Longview area—
Little Colorado Block's burial will be at Portis Cemetery sometime around
2. The funeral is at Mack's at 1 with the burial to follow. It would be nice
if there were no gun shots at that time.

GEORGE BROWN

I'm sure there are several hunts planned around me here on The Corn Rd.
Not me but others.

DOROTHY GREEN CHALMERS

this precious little boy is the son of Abby and Timothy Block. Abby is Eu-
gene Fowler's niece. He was born at 25 weeks and fought hard for 21 days.
Pray for his sweet family.

DENISE MANN

It would be polite if they would not shoot. At least out of kindness and respect so I'm sharing.

CANDACE D. LARRIMORE

Thanks to all of you it worked. Only a couple of shots were heard and they were far off. Most people probably did not even notice them.

LXXVIII

Two dowagers, friends from girlhood who have lived in Mount Zion
all their lives, drive to Cold Springs to fabric-shop and have lunch:
much-scrubbed elderly dolls, beloved of neighbors, sons, and daughters.

Blue wigs, red dresses, pearls: the image Zora makes as she bobs
a chin above the steering wheel: powdery moon face, wig
jouncing with every pothole. And Pearl, gracile, diffident—

she grins, she agrees; whatever Zora says, she flutters happily.
It is a little past noon. They have ordered the creamed spinach
and the baby corn at the Bluebird's Rail and polished it off with

Mary's excellent apple pie à la mode, and now as they drive
        through woods
and fields, the progressions of shade and the cool air inside the car
are of a high order of satisfaction. Pearl Ponder. Zora Neatsfoot.

A hill, a bridge, then a valley. When men imagine them like this,
they do not have two fates. They move like halves of a bivalve,
and the thing about to happen, if it has a tail, does not wag;

if it has a voice, does not speak; it waits like dryness for a well
and takes place quietly and remains like the moot eyes of a blind girl.
Zora lets Pearl off by the steps, farewells, backs up, and turns around —

the story of the Cadillac clipping Pearl and dragging her up Sand
    Mountain
ends by two gas pumps at Fountain Bluff. Accident, tragedy,
Hollywood loves flattening to farce. Zora points under the car.

"A noise," she says, and the station boy brings his creeper.
Pearl was not brilliant, but mention any pain, she would
brighten and say, "I, too, have suffered from that complaint."

L X X I X *(Rumors About Dread Mills)*

At last they have him in church, a short service and the family silent, but
the moments after the funeral are like a test.

True: The new base-tube press at Lockland Copper weighed sixty-seven
tons. When they had completed the building and brought it in the door,
six engineers agreed they would have to lift the roof to get the crane in
and lower it into the pit. He heard from Tip Smith, a drinking buddy, a
welder on the job, and wrote the board, saying he would do it for $10,000.
Went to the ice plant, ordered eighteen blocks, filled the pit, rolled the
press onto the ice; then, as the ice melted, pumped out the water.

True: Drunk every day for sixteen years. *False*: Mostly home brew or
moonshine.

True: Every morning Maurice Orr's rooster pissed him off. *False*: He
caught the rooster in a sack, dug a hole behind the house, buried it with
just the neck and head sticking out, cranked the mower, and mowed the
lawn.

False: The story that, besotted on the back lawn, he ordered Jawaharlal to dance and choreographed the steps with a Colt revolver (*Gunsmoke*).

True: Jawaharlal inherited his logic gene, argued when he called him "Jerry."

False: He never hit a lick at a snake. Once he pruned the grapevine. Twice, after midnight, he picked roasting ears from Lionel Spence's garden.

True: When the money from the press job ran out, he wrote bad checks until his name was posted on the glass doors of every business from Cold Springs to Decatur. It hit him one day: go from store to store, copy all the names, print the list of deadbeats twice a year, and sell subscriptions to each store for $50.

True: His *Deadbeat Protection Flyer* took off before passage of the Credit Protection Act. Drinking Jim Beam in the air over Georgia and Louisiana, he was a sloppy man who made a million dollars.

True: The gay son home from Palo Alto. The wife a Holy Roller in a sari. His brilliant, inebriated, redneck math scratched in the chicken yard. The liver. The heart—details

of the unannotated life: grease prints on *Combinatorics*, unused tickets to see Conway Twitty

—CliffsNotes for Abyss Studies—

His mind at the end like a hand reaching for a pocket when he wasn't wearing a shirt.

"I would kill myself if there were anyone better."

The Ladies' Auxiliary presents the winners of the Cold Springs Art Show in late April in the armory behind the high school. A warm day, everyone smiling up from the folding chairs set out in three rows on the concrete floor.

Scholarly applause as Marie Spence approaches the lectern and stops as she stops each year and looks up, scrutinizing the American Legion banner.

As if the two perennial finalists were not sitting behind her.

Turpentine competing with gun-oil from last night's National Guard meeting.

"Art," she says, "the beautiful thing!" And calculates a cough that decrescendos into laughter. "Well, you either get it or you don't."

Yet there are those unhappy here, feeling the hardness of the seats.

And lined up like crucifixion cuts on one wall: twelve bowls of fruit; little fisherman sleeping under tree, pole propped on stone, gesso waves whitecapping from the cork; a freckled, pigtailed girl; jam face; bay horse with sprig of violets in its mane; barns; cats; etc.

Because even the most exacting craft gets one only so far.

Because a geisha is an art person, all people their art.

Because if there are two of you, the second is less valuable.

The stage light shines only on the finalists: Willadean Byars stark in long-sleeved black blouse and long dress, her hair swept back from her face and falling clean to the waist in a straight braid. Lionel Spence, Marie's husband: the breeze, the formidable jackass.

The four medals secret in the velvet box on the table beside Marie as four veils are lifted and winners revealed.

COPPER: a nude, an egg tempera of an African Gray: standing in its own feathers, it looks out of an oven with the cheeky pout of a state-line stripper; its punctum is a middle-aged pouch; on one leg, a fishnet stocking; on the other, a gray wedding ring strung to *Bay of Banderas, 5 April 1973.*

BRONZE: watercolor of a millrace: sluice gates open, ripples on the surface, autumn water of orange leaves and gossamer, but underneath a head—drowning perhaps was the implication, but gazing up at you calmly, a shark's eyes in a woman's face, fixed in its look and not troubled in the least.

SILVER: an oil painting, it is a chicken. Based on Titian's *Conversion of Constantine,* it struts like an emperor in the emerald of its own excrement as it scratches behind one ear; one wing feathered, the other steel, emblazoned *Spence S-100 Egg Machine.*

GOLD: a portrait: dark colors, the figure neither old nor young, a woman seated at walnut table in plain black dress with white fringe at neck; a single tear seems to be falling from the left eye, but a hand holds it above the table in a gold caliper, and in the air beside it, in cramped calligraphy, *1 ench* and *Rennaisance!*

For each painting, one word: *intriguing, character, Soutine, gold.* Art. One smile on Marie's face, many teeth in her eyes.

LXXXI *(Lionel Spence)*

Bed he will never sleep in again

A Lion, a Mason, a Kiwanian,
the public life of board memberships,
presidencies, and when he passed
early Saturday morning,
a massive coronary
under the most salaciously
indecorous circumstances
with a Dolly-Partonish Miss Flagg
in a rented room of the west wing
of the Mulberry Motor Lodge,
and when she had duly wept,
smoked three Benson & Hedges,
composed herself,
and rang the hospital,
the ambulance came
and took away the body.

Bed to which he returned
many nights sea-legged sump
and stinking of salt mackerel

A pretty drive in spring,
corn just sprouting
in black fields
above the river,
churches and graveyards,
mares and foals,

clutches of wildflowers
beneath mossy bluffs;
the fording of the creek,
going and coming back,
things that must be seen
to put the body in perspective.
At the city limits,
the driver hollers
out the window to a neighbor,
the brick part of town,
and then the hospital,
orderlies rushing out.

Bed of divagations of mutinies captain's bed
Herman Melville could have written that bed

The doors slide open:
pellucid aluminum light;
a few men placing
compresses over cuts
on hands and arms
an old woman who
has fallen, complaining
to her nephew's wife
about the Indian doctors;
the young meth addict,
a bruise over one eye—
the wheels squeak
and the gurney rolls by.
The body in that hour
when the blue

takes on that waxy pallor
is like an egg sent back
to the kitchen in the diner.

Bed from which wife
rose answered phone
dressed drove
straight to the poolroom
and placed a bet

The hours pass. Well,
men say, Well, by God,
it does not require
a rocket scientist
to reckon, he's dead all right
and sign the certificate,
and it scratches no itch,
this is Mr. Lionel Spence
and not just any idiot.
But Mr. Mack himself
does not usually drive
the ambulance from
the funeral home,
and the sheet on the body
is not usually so white.

Bed where she lay with his ghost
rubbing a green jelly bean
salvaged from her morning
tea with Ronnie Reagan.

A new sheet—why
do Americans respect

the rich?—Mack
ponders this and
on the sheet, a gilt
card embossed
Mrs. Lionel Spence,
the message penned
beneath, his mother's
quotidian edict to the help:
Don't wash, he'll
only get dirty again.

LXXXII   *(The Beauty of Young Women in Small Towns)*

Now Luck sees them all, short and demure or tall and regal,
The gawky and homely stages,
And how and when they became beautiful,
The long hair in the eyes, the eyes slightly averted,
The smooth brown thighs against white shorts.
Many were beautiful only for a few seconds,
Sometimes in winter, cheeks reddened by frost,
Often in early summer,
Sad and alone, sitting in the shade of a ginkgo,
Or bristling on the board
Before diving into the pool.

In that instance, if another young woman noticed
And spoke of it, and the others agreed,
They became known as beauties.

And this would not change if they broke out in sores
Or put on sixteen pounds. If one eye
Began glancing off to the side or one breast
Drooped beneath the other, they went on
Being noted for the special quality of their beauty:
Maids of cotton, homecoming queens,
Princesses of peaches or apples.

But if Luck noticed a young woman's beauty and spoke of it,
He was disregarded: that, quite suddenly,
He blushed and stammered when she entered a room
Was of no consequence — he was a young man,
After all, blinded as all males are blinded.
And the young woman — once she had been cited
By a young man as beautiful, she had no status after that —
She was like a box with nothing inside —
There was no reason to look any further.

And everyone knew the rules of this game.
For a young woman to be beautiful,
The young men had to agree with the young women
That she was beautiful,
And before they agreed, they had to be told.
Once the young men were told, nonbeauties
Were free: to stay, to leave. In the future,
Perhaps in Milan or Paris, someone might see
The high cheekbones, the startling eyes,
And say *ecco* or *voilà*. But here they had no names.

Shadow dancers, church sweepers, waitresses
In eternal diners: *How long?* they wrote

In diaries, and *Bumfuck, drizzle, nothing happened.*
Sometimes their phones would ring late Saturday night,
But if they answered, silence. Already
The young men spoke of them as though they were far away:
Stars shining out there on the first nights of spring;
Governesses on mythical commonwealth islands,
Unapproachable in the actual world,
Suitable only for literature.

━━

(1974–1989, 2015)

ONLY THE ANIMALS ARE REAL

LXXXIII *(Chanterelles)*

Black trumpets, whale-colored pamphlets, or shingles, or ears, book-
marks of the netherworld, breakfast food of the box turtle.

For a long time, she could not find them, hovering just above them
the way an inanimate lamp will hang blindly above the lucidities
of geometry.

And then she saw them risen in clusters on the mossy rocks, firm and
articulate, as when first translated from the original rain.

Bat wing, toad mask, vole shield: they turned darkly in the alchemy of
the skillet—in the mouth, they transmit a tenuous signal,

a hint of perfume, but musical—songs with morals, light things broad-
cast before the planetary news on the underground station.

LXXXIV

Sunday morning and Brown worries about the silence of his squirrels. While he chatted with friends on the porch last night, the young father or mother leapt onto a dead branch and fell with the branch a good twelve or fifteen feet. It merely shouted *goddam* and scurried home, and still no noise from their pine. They have not seemed churchgoers. A headstrong couple since the days of their madcap courtship, when they chased each other from roof to treetop, bickering and squalling like any cousins in love. Then, of course, they did what mating animals do after the ritual displays or the fights in discotheques. They built their nest. He follows them, though they are not even people. He hopes they are alive.

LXXXV

Mann regarded his man-selves. Drastically. Mann addled. Mann indigo. Mann challenged by man-hubris and man-baggage sang to the portal in the bathroom vanity. The dewlaps under his chins vanished. Mann the tiger endorsed his man-animus, his man-shadows. Elegiac Mann raised his brow to topmast. Mann down sang to Mann up. Mann out to Mann in. Mann quicksand to Mann aurora borealis. Mann the old man saw Mann the boy. In Jakarta, on the twentieth of May, whitening his teeth, dyeing his hair. Mann loved himself in spite of the age difference and the language barrier.

LXXXVI

Ticks have no virtues unless the hedge of irritation they sow on labia and scrotum be also moral hedge against pornography. Hard cases, addicts, intimate apocrypha, ticks mark the spot where creation got out of hand

and God stopped. For they have made unto Luck a place where he stoops as in a perverse prayer and peers between his legs at the mirror image of his own backside. The tiny ones do not devour streptococcus. The large ones, rubies on the spines of bird dogs, will not excrete cures for lupus or impetigo. Still, he honors their night. Body scratching itself in sleep, conscious mind hovering like a kid with a remote control. So creeps the ancient hope that suffering embellishes the soul.

LXXXVII

Dogs of the world, anonymous wanderers, moral conundrums, they gather by the road, scavenging milk cartons thrown from the bus: feist pups galled with mange, old hounds, blind and lame, at the end of their utility. Such he once whispered secrets to and begged to keep and was commanded to lead into the woods to execute and bury. And his father was not a cruel man. And Saint-John Perse wrote, "I had a horse. Who was he?" Strays, indigents, souls in fur. Brown's favorite channels the spirit of Veronica Franco. Veronica Franco or Marie Duplessis. She is orange, small, and elegant, a golden Lab–beagle mix. He does not know why she visits. He does not feed her, and she is not his dog.

LXXXVIII

Nothing more casual than a cow. A stained sweatshirt for eyes. Mud-lathed, scuff-marked hocks. A breathing, edible log. Unassuming. Un-prepossessed. Bossy. The constable tail swishing flies takes no note signing the pie-plop behind. Sublime nonchalance. A browsing and musing on the verge of sleep. Then annoyance after a nap. A put-upon nun. No jazz in those horns. A cast die for the grass in its extrusion to milk and meat. Also covenant maker. Black Baal smelted of timothy and clover. Sacrifice penned and driven. A bondage. An acropolis. Her language does not sound like but means *moo* or *leave me alone* or *come hither, calf* or *holier than thou.* Cow. Corn, her Judas and chocolate.

LXXXIX

Coco rings four times and answers herself, "We're not home right now. Please leave a message after the beep." And beeps. Then whistles a little —like Nestus Gurley—a note or two that with a note or two would be a tune. And also sharps the beeps of a garbage truck backing up, says, "C'mon," asks, "How are you?" and answers, "I'm fine. What?" Gray suit, red tail feathers, call girl—whatever you imagined hearing, listen again —if you mean to swing, listen less deeply. Become echo, redux, rain, bark, gear, love cry, and diesel. Exalt. Let go of meaning.

XC

Skink, gram of mania, animated pepper, shadow-monger dressed in panic, monitor of ghostly footfalls, it concentrates in its essential tic the frog leg dropped into oil and the human shock at the verge. If it would stop and let her look, she might imagine the tropic where it hangs in a hammock between two popsicle sticks admiring the iguana's stealth, but it does not stop. Hawk-dodger, crow-pretzel, gallows' twitch. Spider-shark. Porter of readiness, miller of the steady shudder, peripatetic rectitude, run by the power of the sunlit rock, it fortifies Darwin and the idea of being late and the missed appointment. With its blue tail, it reminds her: it will go on. It will not stop.

XCI

She made a barrier with a square of hog wire, set it on the lawn above
the spot where the blandishing turtle laid her eggs, and marked it with
feather and stick—

So he would think to mow around it—and came back and bent down
the edges to thwart raccoons. Everything should be made as simple as
possible, said Einstein, but no simpler.

What he did out in the world was his own business, with animals, with
stocks and bonds, with girls in bars. Not that he was negligent. Only he
needed to think.

She did not have to think, all summer watering that place the way
she folded cutlery inside napkins and left them at the center of plates
for servants.

XCII *(Luck Considers the Difficulties of His Art)*

The eagle above the house, which on further inspection turned out to be
a vulture, remains an eagle in his aria.

For years it has been eagle. To change it back to vulture would only
remind him how rarely facts matter.

To the dead, for instance, or philosophers in love with universal likeness.

Wings circle overhead. Rings soar inside a tree. Often, wrote Rilke,
angels make no distinction between the dead and living.

Luck sits in the yard and listens. The cardinal must have eaten some-
thing remarkable. All it wants to do is sing.

How quickly they came to their full bodies and never that protean instant of metamorphosis, only one day both were inexplicably large with the downy, white, otherworldly mien of the working children of the Depression Thomas Wolfe described as cottonheads.

But one fluffing up and flexing, leaping and beating its wings, while the other hung back, shadowed and tentative. Perhaps because it had hatched later. Or was that its nature, to watch? The sneak, the thief, who watches and conceals as he had waited in the shadow of his sister.

A few weeks, as May turned to June, he studied them through expensive binoculars, then noted in a cheap black notebook events that stood out: mornings, a parent carrying a snake, thunderstorms, hot nights—and what might have transpired in the back of the nest. Killing lessons, lockings of beaks.

Each day a further emergence, until the one he called Jupiter was boldly venturing along high limbs, and the other, the peeker, who remained unnamed, stepping forth in increments, pausing to check the position of its feet and wings as if monitoring gauges for oil pressure or altitude.

Later, when they had first flown and he had missed it, he grieved, though of course, hawks are not people; flight is what feathers are for; eyases fly —badly at first: aiming to soar, they often dip, then flap, flap desperately to clear the eaves. Yardbirds, they grub two weeks. Luck noted, *They apprentice, before becoming hawks, as chickens.*

XCIV *(Luck and the Coyotes)*

What he feared was far off, and what he relished near, so he asked neighbors what they were, and a woman said they were mean, small but tricky creatures. They had lured her daughter's kitty into the woods, then eaten it. No one could stop them. Like migrants they passed along hedgerows and fence lines, but never directly in front of you, and he had not truly seen them until he found one freshly killed: so large the body, so broad the tail, he could not believe it was real, it was knowledge, but no, he did not know yet. He knew when he heard them singing. Knowledge was not the body, but the singing. O the note and O the theme repeating. And the chorus then, the laughing tears. Rimbaud in the barn in Charleville, the opium blowing *Une Saison en Enfer*. Coltrane playing outside. The place where she changed. *Giant Steps*. The truth he heard sometimes and knew false and kept secret because it might be true.

XCV

Moss, exemplary machine of function and beauty, unchanged for forty million years and sponging just enough moisture from the air above the escarpment to form without thought an emerald pallet, how could you care about the pastor of the Rock Springs Holiness Church as he bends and gathers the living proof of faith into an ancient gunnysack? Stepping delicately around your face, a name giver like Adam, he is staid and rational. Because the white of the new Holstein bull's left side resembles a map of the South American continent, he calls him Atlas. Once a rooster named Genghis Khan pecked out his aunt's eye. Once a sow named Rosie nursed an orphan puppy. The mule Horatio does not forgive or accuse the tractor. Untrembling, unfearful, and unkind moss, the pastor wonders about you as the signs progress to apocalypse. Hearing a noise late at night, he wakes, circles the house, and, finding nothing but a coon jimmying the lid of a plastic can, remembers, before returning to bed, to refrigerate the serpents he will pass out to the congregation.

XCVI

Mack's boat comes on fast around the bluffs, so by the time he sees her fishing and cuts the engine, it is already too late to apologize for the twenty-first century.

Clearly he has offended the ancients and is shamed, but as she packs her body under her wings and lifts off, *grark,* she says blithely, so he takes taunt, and flashes, and yells *aiiee.*

And turns quickly. And, finding no witness, auditions a number of moot epistemological tropes and unemployed kennings like *heron person* and *great blue human.*

But as the pulley of the invisible starts hauling her up and across the lake, *grark* she calls again, and again he hollers *aiiee,* and thinks less of her as she alights

in the crown of a dead sycamore and fluffs herself up with regal emphasis, so he will understand their relative positions in the higher order.

XCVII

A young female gray fox in the shadow of the toolshed at the back of the yard chasing then lunging at ghosts.

Who seemed easy with her life and only mildly aloof among rank strangers not even her own kind, trotting near and wheeling to freeze for an instant and hear Brown's whispered "There, there," and "Come closer, friend."

Like wind bristling in a tree. But she is not a friend.

Trapped, drugged, taken in a cage on a truck from the den she had made under the round house by the lake, she wakes the same day in a strange forest by a distant lake.

The rain on her coat is a portal to Wall Street. Her dugs, still strutted with milk for her dead kits, accuse him of a vain complicity.

Men who anthropomorphize the economy as the ice caps shrink.

The currency dealer who weeps at *The Fox and the Hound*, dry-eyed at his mother's funeral.

The retired teacher who dresses her cat in a sweater, but will not send her daughter $600.

This, too, Doctor Charm, Madam Tenderness, George Brown. Things see you coming. Don't baby-talk the monkey.

XCVIII

The opossum, that prehistoric pocket isolette, when headlit, shuts like a politician who shifts topics on being asked a leading question.

Or becomes a hip postmodern possum, her deadpan lump undertaken on the lam, her role of a lifetime nailing a lesser actress attempting her shining self.

A bump where swamp and freeway intersect, Wednesday, a jot past midnight, car-crossed, moon-washed, the instant passing like a wand across a blacktop that was voted on.

And then it lies so still, unmaking beginning as Brown heads uphill. A closed water park. Joe's Imperial Boom City! And farther, going little towns of operettas and pretty-baby pageants. Apolitical

miles between American cities, neither pepper nor salt, where Brown tries not to veer as he considers dinner options: perhaps some golden fries, some fish, and still no exit that is not opossum.

XCIX *(Portis and the Doe)*

One of the deeply shy, one of the abject and baffled, just before twilight she appeared not twenty feet from him, looked him in the eye, and hightailed it back into the trees. Then he remembered how she had come to him first as a human being. Afraid, incoherent, drunk, she had just snapped on the light, stumbled to his bed, and shaken him awake. There, yet not there. Wrong, wrong, wrong, he remembers thinking. The head swayed, wild eyes stared down at him. Then she screamed, "Asshole, you're not even him!" And disappeared. The room was iron. The smell of whiskey hung there like a beard. Oh, he knew her all right: the candor of her body—the wilderness of her mind justified high fences. But who was *he*? What kind of animal?

(1974–2015)

BUENAS NOCHES

C *(Ouroboros)*

What he knows that she does not know is a weapon.
What she knows that he does not know is a style.

What he knows that he does not know is a woman.
What she knows that she does not know is the swan dive.

In their favorite bar the shrimp are flown in daily.
They dance. The whiskey in their feet is six years old.

And when they try to talk? This is what fucking is for.
What he does not know that she does not know is not

What she does not know that he does not know.
Admit he is different from the right-hand metronome.

While she chugs up the mountain, singing "I think I can,"
he kneels to the sensei. He waits. He does not swerve.

Her hips are his learning curve. He is the acolyte
in *Zen and the Art of Archery*, learning as he polishes the bow.

What he imagines he knows she does not have to imagine.
What she imagines she knows but does not know he imagines:

as she was described, walking by the Seven Falls Road
with her blouse tied around her waist, by a previous lover.

What he wants to know is what she wants to forget.
What she knows he wants is what he wants but shouldn't.

Oh, do not say it is sad. It is exactly as happy as it is sad.
The gift is perishable, as the nights thaw into mornings.

His mind like a flower under snow. The cheek and purring
of her Siamese, of which he has dreams, but no memory,

and the mystery as they groomed at the same vanity,
some loneliness he wants to gift unlonesome things.

CI *(The Idea)*

That modern love might be conceived as a video game
is noted in 1992 on the road from San Miguel to Pozos
after Portis waits for a funeral march — the mourners
tote a tiny coffin — but before the burro and cart
backing up a long line of tractor-trailers, a hot day,
the Sierras in the distance blurred by fog and dust.

And forgets why he is here under the auspices
of Spence International and Industria Avícola
to write a tract on Mexico's first totally integrated

automated poultry processing plant. And thinks
instead, "Love germinates in delay," "Love *un poco loco*,"
"Love is the suicide's grave under the nettles."

From time to time, things seem to him worth saving
and he pulls off the road, parks, and jots them down:
Love category: come-on lines that didn't work:
"Didn't my father use to know your mother?"
"Come on, baby, let ol' Mother Nature take over."
Compliment: "Who taught you Tibetan throat singing?"

Saguaro in arroyos, mesquite lining dried rivers.
Sometimes he cannot stop. He holds things in his head.
"Love the game; love like football: ambulance
in one end zone, parents worried and clapping;
love the leading rusher, love polishing the balls,
carrying the towels, love on the bench, substitute loves."

And sees in Pozos frescoes still visible on the standing
walls of the villa destroyed by the earthquake,
Love in the Ruins where Caruso sang for the owners
of the silver mine "Una furtiva lagrima."
Love category: come on lines that did the trick.
That modern love might be conceived as a video game.

As Portis walks the hills behind falling haciendas,
he stoops at the adit of the old Indian mine. It twists
like ideas he is auditioning: that he is Dante,
and the man ahead with the flashlight, his Virgil,
is Samuel Beckett. Sometimes he cuts the flashlight,
the better to see the nothingness that abides

like slaves' picks cracking rocks in shining dinnerware.
That modern love might be conceived as a video game.
The setting might be here; when the light returns
the shaft is dark and deep. Portis takes a rock, drops
it, and counts, as it descends, ideas that will not work.
10–9–8–7–6: the hole with no bottom is one of those ideas.

CII *(The Stunner, the Killer, the Stripper, the Eviscerater,
the De-lunger, the Chiller)*

Now Portis sees the things he has written revealed.
More an odor than a mist rises around the 400 women,
anonymous in white smocks and rubber gloves,
the machines like some stainless-steel premonition
of suburban kitchens, and the birds moving and stopping,
hung by their feet like laundry above the women.
An engineer hands him a smock and rubber boots.
That modern love might be conceived as a video game.
The birds moving and stopping above the women.
There were thirteen of us. My father was a whistler.
Fine-looking man. He had a whistle for each of us.
Please place the chicken in the bag with the milk.
Eleven lines compete, 20,000 chickens a day.
The machines emit raw chunks of data. Computers
establish quotas. Each woman has a bird number.
Dora hums and picks a gizzard out of a carcass.
There is a different stopping time for each station.
The engineer explains, it is all run by computers, *preciso*.
If a woman takes too long, she presses a button.
One computer tells another computer, things freeze.

Expensive, but unavoidable. We look for signs.
The morning sickness if they don't say *embarazada*.
A whiteness around the mouth means glue-sniffing.
The plant, over *arroz con pollo*, in Beckett-speak—
the plant would be perfect if there were no people.

CIII   *(Portis Brainstorms on the Day of the Dead)*

The floats pass: San Juan de la Cruz a sugared skeleton,
Teresa de Jesús astonishing beard and décolletage.
But there are many forms of love to consider,
and any game he might invent has been made better
by game-meisters one cannot hope to emulate.
Now sundry brilliances pop up only to vanish,
as the cunnilingus metaphor "yodeling in the canyon"
was eclipsed by "talking to the boat people."
"Gun-show love: fellows in the Old Testament,
a rowdy, horny, homicidal bunch, would love
these little Rugers, and the Glock is hot. It is like
being locked in a box with a Victoria's Secret model."
Junior Spence saying, "Quality, Efficiency, Economy,"
Mann asking, "What do lesbians bring to a second date?"
"Love perky, yes, I would definitely say perky."
"Love David and Jonathan in the Old Testament."
"Love the blind mare returning to the mound
by the creek where they buried the gelding."
The idea that modern love might be conceived of
as a video game justifying itself: "But any halfway decent
American imagination hires a butler and Sherpa."

"Love, the funeral whore." "One night *amor*,
next morning a voice on machine: Were you
completely satisfied with your visit to our boudoir?"
The floats pass, he fetches the pencil and strikes,
looking down from a window dreaming of love,
the game dead burlesque of hearts that mattered
as stars come out and cold the night and cold
the game, more or less one foot in the grave
between the bald barber and the starving cook.

(FIVE POSTCARD CRITIQUES OF THE EARLY THINKING)

MAY 15

Hello Limuel, fantastic stuff here, but knock knock, what the fuck, it is 19-fucking-92. Like Dorothy, this is not Alagodambama. Dare I suggest images, even characters? Start in Boomer. Maybe make your penises Elmer Fudd and your vaginas Jerry Garcia. Transpose to Gen X. Come forward. Think future. I mean who plays this shit: 11–15 year old boys. We're talking fucking children, Limuel. It must be must be visual. It must be violent and dirty.

Besos, Bro,
Jawaharlal and Raymond

p.s. Not that it clicks, game-wise, but Raymond digs the funeral whores.

MAY 21

What's the deal, Goober? Like Junior Spence won't pay your greens fees. A video game? I'd say conceived but fetal. Dig the sissy pistols, but go bigger. Plutonium ray guns. Flying cars with bionic fins. Watch Highlander.

Big oil loves itty bitty chickens.

But seriously,
Dudley "Big" Mann

June 4

Lose the silver mine. Maybe play with meat market. Animals in Gold's Gym. Studs at the iron pile. Foxes at hot yoga. All wrapped in spandex. Think ripped. No, better yet, restaurant. Think candlelit. Some are prime rib. Others graze from steaming plates. Don't be so goddam prissy. Forget Sam Beckett. Always with you, too much Keats. Think Homer Simpson channeling Chaucer's "Methinks a lady hath no beard." And dating has evolved. Black people, gay people. Seriously, bub. It's hard these days. Maybe some gay stud with straight chicks.

A quarterhouse sitting down to a porterhouse.

Never,
Lonely

JUNE 9

Pandering to masturbation with funeral whores. Seriously, Seth, now that Bill Clinton's Franco, look for allowable moisture in frozen fryers to rise and FDA standards on potentially carcinogenic vaccines? History. Not just what chickens do for us, things we do to them: hormones, five-year-olds in Argentina, breasts like Hustler freaks. The horror, Seth, the pity. Fuck Junior Spence. Try reading Bly, Chomsky. Ask yourself what Jesus would think about your game. Think for once about the consciousness of chickens.

Siempre familia,
George and Milly

JUNE 22

Modern love? Try Mrs. Grimmer buck naked on an embalming table, neck arched, head locked in rigor mortis. Make me not think. Crawl your rooster back into the dumplings. Back feelings good. But much simpler, much crazier please pass the goddam catheads. Of course, I do see what you mean. Buena suerte.

Buenas noches and Déjà vu,
Mack Mack (Mack Daddy)

Buenas Noches, the game of love, male heterosexual version

(parts of three levels and five moods)

comes to Portis as he walks the killing floor

with pencil and pad, tweaking the galley

of *Mexico's First Totally Integrated Automated*

Poultry Processing Plant, a warm day

the morning after his mother calls to ask,

"How you doing this glorious evening, sunshine?"

"Okey-dokey, dealing with it, a little bummed by chickens."

Alice, the woman who dumped him, made self-portraits.

She ran a gym called Bodacious Bends.

The machines like some stainless-steel premonition

of suburban kitchens, and the birds moving and stopping,

hung by their feet like laundry above the women.

In the first level you must choose an avatar:

Rock Star, Bodhisattva, Cowboy, Nerd.

To proceed to the level of erotic sustainability,

you must pass through the vale of tortures.

More an odor than a mist rises up around the 400 women,

anonymous in white smocks and rubber gloves.

The moods are genies: music, colors, hormones,

ocean, or night sky. Vacuumed from trucks,

stunned, killed, and plucked,

the headless bodies move like nudes in a pageant.

Breasts, legs, thighs. Love needs a honky-tonk.

Players may find the moods on the jukebox.

A popular choice is "Smells Like Teen Spirit."

Another, "The sun is not yellow. It's chicken."

The game is simple. Avatars battle avatars.
Avatars are not permitted to speak. People
with breasts but no last names say "Buenas noches."
Eleven lines compete, 20,000 chickens a day.
The machines emit raw chunks of data.
Love needs hints. The hinters are Darwin and Iago.
The queen of love who comes out of the sea
and speaks all languages is Venus then Helen.
Cher purrs in a basket. When the Bodhisattva leans
to rub her, she shape-shifts to Medusa. Computers
establish quotas. Each woman has a bird number.
Dora hums and picks a gizzard out of a carcass.
She is the widow of a species who mates for life,
and Iago says: "When the husband dies
a new partner is generally found the succeeding day;
but Mr. Thompson gives the case
of one being replaced on the evening of the first day."
Babies are transformers. Each bears a sign. *She
Has Found Someone Better.* Vulnerability scores.
Bonus points earn interviews with Darwin.
The Cowboy's question: Bolo tie? Enter Darwin:
"A female zebra would not admit the addresses of a male ass
until he was painted so as to resemble a zebra,
and then as John Hunter remarks, she received him
very readily. But the male did not require this."
In the game, as in the plant, everyone watches
herself being watched on hidden cameras.
When Alice said, "Needs not being met," he saw his avatar:
a riderless horse bucking an empty saddle.
The game coming into shape in the portal,

according to the precepts of modern
chivalry and ancient pornosophy,
in the zeitgeist of Cobain and Love,
Portis writes the box copy for Buenas Noches
above the Spence International signature,
Economy, Efficiency, Quality:
Brief frontal nudity, violence, portals inside portals.
Lose, you drop down a hole.
Win, you will not be permitted to play again.
Soon all core gamers will queue for the sequel.
Now, if only Mills will write the code.

CV

Unvisualized Sunday, subfusc and far away.
Teak and holly in the galley,
Veuve Clicquot, fresh basil on sliced tomatoes,
Beluga caviar, Glenn Gould's
Goldberg Variations—the prime
directive of the post-Reagan years,
let nothing impede profit,
has nourished Mills: his boat
is paid for; his partner a surgeon.
When they wake after making love
one brews green tea, the other sings,
Il paradiso, grazie mille, my nigga.
As if the whole day were a passage
sunlight has quoted from Puccini.
The hammocks, the breeze. At home

a message blinking on the machine:
him again, drawling on and on about
that crazy video game. Honey
what the hell is it with Seth Portis?

C V I *(The Portal Leaks)*

The game on hold, the tract a fait accompli,
some ideas coming out, others going in:

> Portis alone in bed the third night sleepless
> measures degrees of darkness as it drops
> chakras of clarity in the bougainvillea,
> hears *parakeet genius*   thinks *roosters*
> *plagiarize infinity,*   hears *astro-vaginal physics*
> thinks *hole in my heart,*   hears *laminate Jesus*
> thinks   *now commenceth the holy ridding.*

The old ideas as they leave sound like boxes locking
in the vaults and the banker looks up from the treasure.

> The queen of love who comes out of the sea
> and speaks all languages is Venus then Helen.

Or is it Cher saying *Buenas noches* to the congressman?

> Morning sensuality at the conference table
> Portis dips his orange roll in fresh arabica.

Cracking open the morning with a gavel,
Junior Spence, CEO of Spence International,
as he initials the final proof of *Mexico's First*

Totally Integrated Automated Poultry Processing Plant,
is the spitting image of his mama.

Or is it Cher saying *Buenas noches* to the congressman?
The walls with their dust noise. A ginkgo crosses the table.

The ego is fractured when one perceives
An inner vision as an exterior mass.
    Nearly inconceivable Portis scribbling
    love the wrong thing to say to police.

The Stunner, the Killer, the Stripper,
the Eviscerator, the De-lunger, the Chiller
in Portis's mind change from machines to women.
    He mumbles, *ineluctable morality of the risible.*

Thinks what is recent? What is *incidentalism*? The trouble

in his mind cracks the bell in the *parroquia.*
    A day distinguished by latencies and temporal bleeds.

    He walks and what is a walk? There. Here. Again.
Until they sedate him and pack him with Junior on the Lear.

At Rosedale, in Birmingham, he comes to, eyes fixed
on Haldol heaven, and forgets why or what
he twists the restraints and strains to resist.
The room and the bushes outside are green.
The world he has hidden in his heart numbs.
The muscles in his arms are twitching Erector sets.
The third morning an orderly leads him to calisthenics.
More a mist than an odor rises from the tray of needles,
nurses in white smocks and rubber gloves.
When he tries to speak, his tongue clucks between his lips.
When a doctor hands him a questionnaire and pencil,
the lead shackles on his mind's feet
are the accumulated weight of thirty
Cold Springs women praying for him.
He shuffles to the men's room. The nurses bring the tray.
Now light hurts. Now lithium shrinks the spectrum.
Often when he shuts his eyes, he sees the white sole
of a foot adrift in space. If he focuses on this foot,
the flesh undulates, and in the waves, an eye appears.
When he describes it, the doctor asks him to draw it.
Everyone is an artist or prophet here.
The pug-painter Mavis, who ran naked through the field,
broke down when her lover stood at assembly,
confessed, and resigned as Sunday school superintendent.
The balding, aquaholic John the Baptist
begs quarters at the drink machine.
The days lighten when Portis hears him.

CVIII *(Portis Recovering)*

Decided, later, he   should, after all,
have considered, when   he instructed Mills
to take a hard right at   the Shell station
instead of left, the   correct direction,
and then another   right at the silo,
when left was right   again, then follow
the creek until he   saw a granite quarry
across from a   nonexistent cemetery,
that this was the   twentieth century,
that systems   spring from the arbitrary,
that Mud Creek clears   in an aquarium
that plus   cancels minus in a dream,
that this was Mills,   not any idiot,
and he would be there in sixteen minutes.

CIX

Portis shrinks.
As Portis shrinks, the world that he contains enlarges.
The voices in his head diminish.
His aspect and his affect wither.

                         And still he is not yet invisible.

But rather about the size of a pea.

For which Doctor Block ventures a fulsome wink.
     The doctor's value increases
     in inverse proportion
     to the smallness of Portis's footprint.

A post-cartoonish treatment, this shrinkage:
each session a needle prick or knot slipped,
and like a bloviating party balloon
a mean confidence goes off hissing   goes off

and lies limp   again   again   again
until Portis deigns not mention
the idea modern love might be conceived as a video game.

A victory. A breakthrough. And still, after the annotated
leakage of three years, not all of Portis is in this:

   inchoate omissions among hangover insights,
quicksilver drips that flicker and disappear.
   Unbowdlerized chronicles of the penis.

Images of guilt and mortification
watched by the secret eye that floats inside the white sole of a foot
that changes to a mountain,
secret unchanging eye in the pyramid on the dollar bill,
mother watching as the sin grows beautiful
before the Zoloft takes,
when the shame grows loveliest.

Though this must never be said. Just so,
from a sweet madness Portis is weaned.

One place is as good as another to be born
and return after years, like Odysseus to Ithaca or mildew to a
rotting plank.

How Sunday it all looks now, paved and pastured, fieldless and storeless.

Burglar music. Late morning. No one home.

And the past, still and under: its sawdust ice, its milk jugs screwed tight
and suspended in spring water.

County life, pre-telephone, without verbs.

Small houses, a quarter of a mile apart, of whitewashed or unpainted
clapboard, each with a well and outhouse.

Larger houses with barns, chicken coops, toolsheds, and smokehouses.
Hounds of some significance. Men. Women. Children.

Nary and tarnation. A singing from the fields. A geeing and hawing.

A voice here and there with a smidgeon of Euclid and a soupçon of
Cicero to hifalute what twanged from across the fence and the other
side of the bucksaw.

Each day of 1953 like a pupa in a chrysalis.

Phenomenology buzzing like wasps in the stripped timbers of
the gristmill.

The road out busting from trace and logging ruts. Now and then a
backfiring Studebaker with its doggy entourage and roostertails of dust.

But less and less in 1954, a mare and wagon, orbited by a yearling colt.

The evolution of the cabin to dogtrot, the boarding up of the hall between the west side's living room, kitchen, and pantry, and the east side's two bedrooms.

Stone chimneys at each end, and on the porch across it, the kitty-holed door to the attic's must, mud daubers, and déjà vu.

A spinning wheel with spavined and missing spokes, a warped sidesaddle, boxes of wooden tools, gaiters, spectacles, dried gloves, shoe lasts, letters from dead to dead.

The cellar beneath it all. Wooden casks, wine bottles dusky and obsolesced by the hardshell feminism of the great Protestant reawakening

that quarried legions of infidels from saloons and brothels and restored them to their families. Portis's own.

Tom Portis's vineyard east of the house, his vines of small sour grapes still strung with rusted baling wire to rotting posts.

His continuance bolstered and intensified should a client void a decade and show up early morning, stumble-drunk, moaning, "Virgie, Virgie."

Prose fragments.

The smokehouse. Hams, shoulders, and side meat interred in separate salt bins.

The hog lot.

The well into which, it has been told, Portis once dropped a Persian cat.

And what is the name of the cat? And what word now from the after?

•

Here are some verbs: woke, saw, stretched, heard, washed, smelled, sat, blessed, ate, listened, rose, waited, walked, felt, shat, dug, meditated, buried, gone

though somewhere, perhaps by some odd fractal of the principle of the conservation of matter, a remnant of the original template holds.

Home odor, unreconstructed, peasant, third world—
"Nostalgia for the infinite," the nearly forgotten Bob Watson called it.

Maybe it's just like that. Maybe it's exactly what they say
after years to the old when they were children.

(1992–2009)

NOTES

Sections II, IX, and XIII of "Requiem for Reba Portis" allude to or make direct use of language from Gerald Edelman's splendid book on consciousness, *Wider Than the Sky*.

At the end of Section XXXV of "Reversals of Fortune," *Stories and Texts for Nothing* is by Samuel Beckett; *The Seven Ages* is by Louise Glück, and *Cemetery Nights* is by Stephen Dobyns, to whom the poem is dedicated.

The last two lines of Section XXXVI of "Reversals of Fortune" paraphrase the closure of Robert Penn Warren's poem "True Love."

Section XL of "Wayward Swains in a Time of War" is for Dave Smith.

Most of Section LX of "The Righteous Trip" is taken from the language of several letters in John Keats's *Letters to Friends and Family*.

Section LXVII of "Puberty in Cold Springs" alludes to the early-1960s television program *The Many Loves of Dobie Gillis*.

The letter alluded to in Section LXIX of "Puberty in Cold Springs" is from John Keats's *Letters to Friends and Family*. The poem is dedicated to Maurice and Amanda Manning.

Section LXXIV (Elegy for the Crooked and Out of the Way) of "Did You See Any of the Others While You Were There" is in memory of C. D. Wright.

The Erdös number mentioned in section LXXVI of "Did You See Any of the Others While You Were There" refers to the status conferred on mathematicians by their association with the great Paul Erdös. Mathematicians who collaborated directly with Erdös were assigned the number 1, while their collaborators were assigned number 2, and so on.

Combinatorics, in Section LXXIX (Rumors About Druid Mills) of "Did You See Any of the Others While You Were There" refers to the journal that publishes articles on the branch of mathematics dealing with the enumeration, combination, and permutation of sets of elements and the mathematical relations that characterize their properties.

Section LXXXVII of "Only the Animals Are Real": Veronica Franco (1546–1591) was an Italian poet and courtesan, the mistress of Franz Liszt, and the subject of Margaret Rosenthal's 1992 book *The Honest Courtesan* and the movie *Dangerous Beauty* (1998). Marie Duplessis (1824–1847) was the French courtesan immortalized in Alexandre Dumas *fils*'s *La Dame aux Camélias* and Verdi's *La Traviata*.

In Section CI of "Buenas Noches," the line "Love is the suicide's grave under the nettles" is from C. Day Lewis's "Departure in the Dark."

In Section CIV of "Buenas Noches," the quoted passages are from Charles Darwin's *The Descent of Man*.

In Section CVI of "Buenas Noches," "*ineluctable morality of the risible*" is a twisting of James Joyce's "ineluctable modality of the visible," from *Ulysses*.

Much of the description in Section CVII of "Buenas Noches" would not have been possible without the advice of the poet and psychiatrist Owen Lewis.

ACKNOWLEDGMENTS

I am grateful to the family of Mary Rogers Field and the English Department of Depauw University for honoring me with the Mary Rogers Field Distinguished University Professorship in Creative Writing, which gave me time to write much of this book, and to the wonderful Lannan Foundation for a residency in Marfa, Texas that allowed me to make significant progress toward finishing it. Thank you Kathleen Balma, Josh Bell, Ralph Adamo, C. D. Wright, Kerry James Evans, Molly Bendall, T. R. Hummer, Ben Downing, David Mills, Javi Jones, Tom Huey, Dave Smith, Stephen Dobyns, Peter Cooley, Andy Young, Brad Richard, Kay Murphy, Carolyn Hembree, and Jenny Xu for invaluable suggestions on earlier versions of this manuscript.

I wish to acknowledge the editors of the following magazines for publishing some of these poems, often in different forms:

Atlantic: X as "Stove." *Blackbird:* "The Portal of the Years," XXXVII as "Making Ready," XLII as "Roommates, 1969," XLIV as "Staying in Cold Springs," LXXXV as "Fable." *Crab Orchard Review:* LXVII as "The Power of the Quote." *Eighteen Bridges* (Canada): LXXXVII as "Strays." *Five Points:* LXI as "The Breaker," LXVI as "The Age of Accountability," LXXI as "The Fastidium," LXXII as "Cold Springs Apostrophe," LXXX as "Lionel Spence." *Kenyon Review:* CX as "Homecoming." *Manchester Review* (UK): LXXXIII as "Chanterelles," LXXXIX as "African Gray," XCIV as "Coyotes," XCVI as "Heron." *New Ohio Review:* LXXIX as "Rumors About Dread Mills." *Oxford American:* XVI, XVII, XIX, XX, XXI, XXIII, XXIV, XXVI, XXVII, XXVIII, XXIX, XXXI, XXXII, XXXIII, XXXIV as "The Secret Order of the Eagle." *Parnassus:* LXXIV (Elegy for the Crooked and the Out of the Way), LXXVI as "Cold Springs in California," LXXVIII as "North Alabama Love Story." *Poetry:* XC as "Skink." *Shadowgraph:* XLIII as "Stretch." *Shenandoah:* XCIII as "Hawks Fledging," XCV as "Moss," XCVII as "Talking to the Animals," XCVIII as "Bump," XCIX as "Portis and the Doe." *Smartish Pace:* XXII as "The Polio Victim," XL as "Parade Grounds," LXX as "Willows," LXXXII as "The Beauty of Women in Small Towns," C as "Ouroboros." *Southern Indiana Review:* LXXVII as "Cleaning the Trap." *Triquarterly:* LXXXVIII as "Cow." *Xavier Review:* LXV as "The Negro Question," LXVII as "A Free Throw in 8th Grade," LXXI as "Hope Came."

"The Power of the Quote" (LXVII) was reprinted in *Hard Lines: Rough South Poetry*, ed. Daniel Cross Turner and William Wright (University of South Carolina Press, 2016).

"Parade Grounds" (XL) was reprinted in *Poetry Daily*.

Alternate versions of nine sections of "Only the Animals Are Real" were published in *Twelve Fables Set in the Shawnee Woods* (Red Iris Press, 2014).